MICHELLE VERNAL LIVES in Christchurch, New Zealand with her husband, two teenage sons and attention seeking tabby cats, Humphrey and Savannah. Before she started writing novels, she had a variety of jobs:

Pharmacy shop assistant, girl who sold dried up chips and sausages at a hot food stand in a British pub, girl who sold nuts (for 2 hours) on a British market stall, receptionist, P.A...Her favourite job though is the one she has now – writing stories she hopes leave her readers with a satisfied smile on their face.

If you'd like to know when Michelle's next book is coming out you can visit her website at www.michellevernalbooks.com[1]

---

1. http://www.michellevernalbooks.com

Also by Michelle Vernal
The Cooking School on the Bay
Second-hand Jane
Staying at Eleni's
The Traveller's Daughter
Sweet Home Summer
The Promise
When We Say Goodbye
The Dancer
And...

The Guesthouse on the Green Series

Liverpool Brides Series

The Autumn Posy
The Winter Posy – out February 2021

The Guesthouse on the Green – Book 9
Due in March
Michelle Vernal

Chapter One
Dublin 2001

'I'm late,' Moira said dumping her satchel down on a spare seat before sitting down at the table opposite her pal, Andrea. They'd not seen each other in weeks but she wasn't here for a cosy catch up.

She took a second to survey the crowded lunch bar and wished Andrea had chosen somewhere quieter to meet for lunch even though she was as partial to their specialty gourmet sandwiches as the next girl.

Sammy's was Andrea's favourite lunchtime spot though. It had been their Friday haunt in the days before Moira had enrolled in art school. They'd used it as their treat to mark the end of the working week. That was when Moira was still employed at Mason Price, the law firm where Andrea ran around after the cantankerous, Nora, queen of the taxation department. The stodge of all that bread had set them up for the after-work drinks sessions in the evenings too.

All of which seemed a lifetime ago now, Moira thought, settling herself into her seat. She sniffed the yeasty smell of freshly baked bread that would, under normal circumstances, have her tummy rumbling in anticipation. Today though the smell left her cold and could have been overcooked broccoli for all that it tempted her.

Andrea raised her head from the menu to greet her friend with a wide grin before glancing across to the wall clock behind the counter.

'You're not late. Well, only a couple of minutes but by your standards, that's pretty good. Isn't it a gorgeous day out there? You'd never guess it's supposed to be autumn with the week we've had. If we had more time it would have been nice to get our sandwiches to take away. We could have found a spot to soak up the sun by the canal. Mind you, the sight of all that pasty Irish male flesh I spotted walking over might put us off. You know what the lads are like. A hint of sun no matter what time of year and they're stripping off like they're lying on a beach in Ibiza. Mark my words, Moira, there will be bad cases of sunburnt chests all over Dublin tonight.'

Moira nodded her agreement. She could almost smell the sizzle of chest hair as they spoke. There'd be a run on the E45 cream for sure.

Andrea was wasting her time perusing the menu, she thought, glancing over at the white card her friend was holding and admiring the pale pink of her nail polish as she did. She could've told her what she was going to order before she sat down. Andrea was a creature of habit. She always had a chicken Caesar wrap with extra mayo. Always.

Moira picked up the salt shaker for want of something to do with her hands. 'No. I mean *I'm late, late.* Two months to be exact, pushing toward three.'

The penny dropped and Andrea's mouth fell open. 'Jaysus, Moira. You're not.' Her brown eyes darted left and right as though there were spies everywhere before she leaned across the table to try and cop a load of her friend's stomach before whispering, 'Pregnant, are you?'

Hearing it said out loud felt like a slap across the cheek and Moira flinched. 'Ah Jaysus, don't be saying the 'p' word, Andrea. I don't know for sure. And stop looking at my belly. Sure, it's three months not eight and I had pasta for dinner last night that's all. You know I blow up on that.'

'Sorry.' Andrea sat back in her seat.

'I keep thinking of reasons I might be late on. You know, too much exercise, stress, that sort of thing.' Moira had been clinging to the hope there was a perfectly valid reason for her monthly not having arrived other than the glaringly obvious one.

'What exercise have you been doing?'

'Only the ridey sort.'

'Obviously,' Andrea said having forgotten all about the menu she'd been staring hungrily at a moment earlier. It lay face down on the table ignored by them both. 'Is it college stressing you out?'

'No. I love college and I'm not stressed. Well, apart from having no money. That stresses me out. I saw a gorgeous dress in the window of Storm Cloud the other day. Remember that boutique you and I checked out when we were looking for dresses to wear to posh Mairead's engagement do?' Her eyes took on a dreamy quality remembering halcyon days spending all of what she earned each week.

Moira had come a long way since that party where she'd made a holy show of herself. She'd given up the sauce for one thing as it had become glaringly obvious she'd a problem with the drink. Now though she'd got herself in another right mess.

She focused on the memory of the dress once more, not that she'd have any need of sexy, floaty dresses if she was, as she suspected, pregnant. No, it'd be a sack she was after.

'Do you mean the pricey boutique on Henry Street that makes you want to clench your bottom cheeks when you step inside it?'

'What do you mean clench your bottom cheeks?' Moira frowned at the imagery.

'I always do it when I walk in somewhere that's really, really expensive. It's reflexive. I think I'm subconsciously trying to brace myself for the shock when I see the price tag.'

'Andrea, that's a very strange thing to do.'

'Do you think?'

Moira nodded. They were getting off track. 'Quinn leaves the toilet seat up all the time, too. That stresses me out. And Aisling's always referring to Quinn as 'my husband'. That's like fingernails down the blackboard each time I hear it which is immensely stressful.' She was surprised at just how much stress there was in her life now that she thought about it.

'But he is her husband.'

'And has been for months and months now. That's the point, Andrea. We know. All of Dublin knows and since we went to Los Angeles, all of LA knows too. It's very annoying her going on like so. Oh, and I get super stressed when I hear the headboard start to bang in their room.' It should be Aisling, not her who suspected she was in the family way. She'd not been shy in announcing she and Quinn had decided to start trying for a family. They'd been trying very, very hard by all accounts. They'd get the gold star for effort for sure.

'I've been spending more and more time at Tom's which isn't ideal because he's got these two eejitty flatmates, Tamar and Malcolm. They're medical students too and honestly, Andrea, they live and breathe all things mediciney. I wouldn't mind if they were after wanting to do something glamorous with their qualifications, you know like the ER on the tele or something but they're both looking at the general practice. I missed a crucial bit on *Fair City* the other night because Tamar was going on about the causes of ingrown toenails.'

'Ooh, she didn't happen to come up with any cures did she? My mam's after moaning about hers all the time. She always brings it up right on teatime too.'

'No, she didn't, sorry.' Moira's thoughts turned to Malcolm. He'd been short with her the other day and yes, alright she'd used the last of the milk and helped herself to his shredded wheat but she hadn't known it was his. 'I think Malcolm thinks I'm a freeloader too.'

'Arse,' Andrea stated loyally.

Moira nodded her agreement. 'He's a specky, fecky arse,' she added, thinking of the black-rimmed glasses he wore. She suspected he didn't need them because he managed to flick through his medical journals without them right enough. He probably thought they made him look like a proper trainee doctor when he wore them. Her Tom was a trainee doctor and he looked like he should be running down the beach in red swim trunks attempting to rescue people. She knew whose bedside manner she'd prefer.

'And did I tell you Mammy and Donal are house hunting? That's the most stressful news of all.'

'For a place together, like?' Andrea gasped at this news.

'Yes. Mammy has decided to live in sin with her man friend.' Moira shook her dark hair. 'There's no stopping her now she's gotten the cast off her foot. I told you she fell off the catwalk in Los Angeles, didn't I?'

'No, you did not. Sure, I'd remember something like that. What was your mammy doing on a catwalk?'

Moira explained how her mammy had announced strutting her stuff down a runway was on her bucket list and how she was convinced she added something new to her bucket list every other week.

'My uncle Cormac's a bigwig designer in Hollywood as you know and he organised for us all to take a turn down the runway prior to a show he was part of. We'd a proper model show us how to walk and everything only Mammy went and ruined it all by strutting right off the end of the thing. She said she was blinded by the lights but I think she got carried away with the ABBA music she chose to be played. You know what she's like. She always has to take things to the extreme.'

It had been a weight off Moira's and Aisling's shoulders to know Mammy had Donal to fetch and carry for her while she was incapacitated with her badly sprained ankle. She was not an easy patient was Mammy. Oh yes, Moira mused, it would have been a true test of Donal's devotion to her mammy, caring for her with a casty foot. Hats off to him, he'd hung in there.

Andrea listened to this story open-mouthed; sure, her family was positively dull by comparison.

'Now she's after ringing me every day with house-hunting updates as if she's on one of those property shows on tele,' Moira said. 'Mammy wants to stay in Howth even though Donal's a Drumcondra man. She says she'd miss not being by the sea now and she loves the holiday vibe of Howth. She thinks she's in the South of France because there's a couple of palm trees that look nothing like the palm trees in Los Angeles so I'm not even sure they're proper palms in the village. I don't think Nice and the likes get arctic gale force winds coming off the ocean either.'

Andrea nodded her agreement. 'Although it's as pretty as anywhere on a sunny day.'

'Sunny, Ireland?'

'Sure, the sun's shining today. It's a scorcher out there so it is.'

'True enough but what's the bet the heavens have opened by four o'clock?'

Andrea hesitated; she wasn't prepared to put money on this.

'She likes to walk Pooh along the pier too. I don't know how he's going to take having male competition under the same roof on a permanent basis.' The poodle still had a propensity for turning into a poodly version of Cujo where Donal was concerned.

'Well I say good for them,' Andrea said. 'I'm all for living your best life.'

'Oh, feck off with you and your women's magazines, Andrea. It's not an episode of Oprah she's after being a guest on. Sure, how would you like it if you knew your old mammy was doing the riding with a new fella?'

Andrea's nose wrinkled. 'I wouldn't like it at all and neither would my dad.'

'Well, I for one think Mammy and Donal are moving very quickly. I mean I know they're not getting any younger but I'd only just got used to the idea of her having a man friend. Now, she's got a man friend who she's moving in with. It's the next step isn't it?'

'Toward what?'

'To me, Ash and Rosi having to wear hideous bridesmaids' dresses, that's what.' Moira's chin jutted up. 'Ah Jaysus, Andrea you don't think Mammy would wear white, do you? Not at her age?' Moira closed her eyes at the mental picture of her mammy in a frothy white princess gown complete with sparkling tiara.

She and her sisters for some reason looked like the ugly stepsisters in the Cinderella book she'd had as a child. It got worse because it wasn't a handsome prince Mammy was after marrying in her polaroid mind-shot but rather Donal who was clad in a white Kenny Rogers suit. It had flared trousers and everything.

A sound bite was added to the film running through her head whereby Mammy and Donal were after singing their vows to the tune of Islands in the Stream. Then things really deteriorated as she realised she was the fat bridesmaid with an enormous belly as she stood alongside her slimline sisters.

'Breathe, Moira,' Andrea ordered.

Moira inhaled deeply and then exhaled. 'I'm getting ahead of myself, aren't I?'

Her friend nodded. 'And no, I don't think she'd wear white. I could see her in red myself. She likes to be different does your mammy. To stand out from the crowd.'

Moira shook her head. 'An understatement if ever there was one.' It was worse than the princess number she decided, thinking of her mammy's favourite Chinese silk red prostitute dress.

'Have you been weeing a lot and throwing up, that sorta thing?' Andrea asked, bringing them back to more pressing matters.

'No, I've not been sick and I haven't noticed I've been going to the loo more. I feel grand in fact.'

'Some women glow all through pregnancy.' Andrea's eyes narrowed as she studied Moira intently. 'You've a glow. Have you not done the pee on a stick thing yet then?'

Moira shrugged. 'No. I'm too scared to because what will I do if the two lines pop up in the window?'

'Well, if you are,' she caught Moira's warning gaze and rethought her terminology, 'in the family way then it's not going to go away just because you decide to pretend it's not happening.' Andrea had forgotten all about her chicken Caesar wrap now. 'What about Tom? Have you told him you're worried?'

Moira fixed mournful eyes on her friend. 'No, he's a lot on his plate at the moment and I don't want to worry him until I know for sure. It's not part of our plans. We're both still students in the throes of our romance,' she said dramatically. 'We're not ready for babies. We can't afford one for starters. I'm having to shop at Penney's these days as it is and besides I'm too young to be a mammy.'

'Not really, Moira, you're twenty-six. You're in your clock ticking prime.'

'Is that right, and what are you doing about your clock ticking prime then?'

'I'm still waiting for Connor Reid to break up with that Amazonian accountant of his and realise his dream woman has been under his nose in the taxation department of Mason Price all along. And don't you be giving out about clocks ticking. My mammy invited her friend Noelle around for tea the other night and they were talking about what a coincidence it was that I was single and so was Noelle's oldest son, Lorcan. Then they went on about how neither of us was getting any younger before trying to psych me out by staring me down. It was very awkward, so.'

'What's he like this Lorcan?'

'He's a face that would drive rats from a barn and I don't want little ratty babies.'

'Fair play.'

'You should talk to Tom, Moira.'

'I don't know how to even start that conversation and it would only make it feel real.'

'You can't bury your head in the sand. Sure, you don't want to be one of those girls you read about who thinks she's getting a little podgy around the middle and then one day she goes to the toilet and there it is.'

'There's what?' Moira eyed her friend warily.

'A baby, you eejit.'

'I've never read that.'

'Well, I have. What would you do if you are? Would you consider a—'

'No.' Moira surprised herself with the certainty of her answer. How she'd manage, what sort of mammy she'd be, and how Tom would take the news were all part of the great unknown but that she'd have the baby if there was one was definite, she was sure. It was more than just her Catholic roots, it was primal.

C'mon, let's skip lunch and go to Boots.' Andrea was already half out of her seat.

'But you said you were starving,' Moira protested.

'I couldn't eat a thing now, not knowing you might be pregnant.'

'I said don't use that word!' Moira scanned the heaving café half expecting to see all eyes had turned to the scarlet woman whose friend had a big mouth.

Everybody was far more interested in their sandwiches than in Moira and Andrea and so Moira slung her satchel across her shoulder and trailed after her pal reluctantly.

Chapter Two

The street they emerged blinking at the bright light onto was thronging with lunchtime shoppers and Andrea, a woman on a mission, was taking no prisoners as she carved a path along the crowded pavement.

'Jaysus, Andrea, you nearly took that poor woman out with your elbows,' Moira muttered trying to keep up.

'I can't stand dawdlers,' Andrea said, suddenly veering right through the doors of Boots.

Moira followed but screeched to a halt just inside the pharmacy's entrance causing the automatic doors to keep opening and closing.

Andrea looked back over her shoulder to see what she was doing.

'Moira,' she said, turning and retracing her steps, 'Hurry up you're interfering with the sensors.' She pointed back at the entrance.

Moira didn't care, she wasn't budging. 'I don't want to buy a test, Andrea. What if I see someone I know? What would I say?'

'Mind your own business, that's what you'd say and would you stop loitering like, it makes you look shifty and we'll get told off for jamming up the doors in a minute.'

'I feel shifty just not in a shoplifter way.'

Andrea sighed. 'I'll buy it, alright.'

'You're a true friend, Andrea.' It was what Moira had been hoping for.

Her friend let out a huffy sigh, 'C'mon then, follow me.'

She could be very bossy, could Andrea, Moira thought, but she did as she was told.

It took them a few minutes to locate what they were looking for because neither girl wanted to ask for help but finally, they were standing in front of the shelf filled with pink and blue boxes with pictures of white plastic sticks with windows on them.

'What do the people who make these things think?' Moira muttered. 'If you choose a blue test kit you're hoping for a boy?'

'I don't know,' Andrea said reaching for a blue box.

'No! Not the blue. If I am you-know-what, you might be tempting fate. We've already got Noah. It's a little girl we need. Take the pink box.'

'But that's dearer and it does exactly the same thing.'

Moira hesitated because while Andrea had offered to buy the kit, that clearly entailed taking it to the counter and handing it over but not the actual paying for it. She'd have to stump up the cash.

'The pink one, Andrea,' She said recalling the time she'd changed Noah's nappy not long after he was born and been piddled on for her efforts.

Andrea murmured something under her breath before picking up a pink pack.

'No, look that one below is cheaper. I'm a student you know.'

'For feck's sake, Moira, you can get it yourself if you're going to keep on and besides it's cheaper because it's only got the one test in it. You want two to be sure.'

'But twins don't run in our family. Sure, I'll only be needing the one.'

Andrea shook her head. Moira's hormones had addled her brain, she thought, plucking the box she'd pointed out from the shelf and heading off towards the counter. She reached the end of the queue, turning to ask Moira for the money to pay for it and frowning. *Where'd she gotten to now?* She retraced her steps and found her perusing the hair colours.

'Why've you a box of ash blonde hair dye in your hand? Sure, you'd not suit the blonde, Moira,' Andrea said sidling next to her.

Moira hissed, 'I don't want to go blonde. Mammy's friend Rosemary Farrell is over there. I knew we'd see someone I know. Don't look and she might not notice us.'

Andrea feigned interest in the box of colour Moira was holding and whispered out the corner of her mouth, 'Are you talking about the woman with the walking pole like they use in the Swiss Alps?'

Moira nodded.

'Jaysus, Moira, all she needs is a Saint Bernard with a whiskey barrel around its neck and she'd be set.'

'It's a hiking pole. She's in Mammy's rambling group.'

Both girls started as a voice sounded behind them and Andrea quickly shoved the pregnancy testing kit in her handbag, zipping it up to be on the safe side.

'Moira, hello there. I thought it was you.'

Moira swung around. 'Mrs Farrell, fancy seeing you here. How are you?' As soon as she asked, Moira knew she was going to live to regret it.

'Well now, Moira, since you ask, my hips after making a peculiar clicking this last while and it's got me worried so it has. Listen...'

Rosemary set off giving them a live demonstration in the Boots' aisle as she strode up and down it with her hiking pole. She'd a sprightly step on her for someone who'd had a hip replacement, Moira thought, watching as Rosemary paused to glare at an elderly man who got in her way. Moira and Andrea held their breath as Rosemary raised her hiking pole in a menacing manner, and it was touch and go for a second or two as to whether she was going to prod him with it. Mercifully, she refrained.

'Mrs Farrell's after having a hip replacement, Andrea,' Moira explained as the older woman returned and both girls made sympathetic noises over the pronounced clicking they'd heard as she'd traversed the aisle.

For Andrea's part, the last vestiges of desire for the chicken Caesar wrap she'd had her heart set on for lunch evaporated upon hearing this appetite destroying sound.

'It's not under warranty is it?' Moira asked.

Rosemary shook her head. 'No, it's a hip, Moira, not an electric appliance.' She proceeded to give them the low-down on the aches and pains which had brought her to Boots.

It was Andrea who butted in. 'I'm sorry to interrupt you Mrs...'

'Farrell. Rosemary Farrell.'

'Farrell, but we're on our lunch break and there'll be murder if we're late back.'

Rosemary's eyes narrowed and homed in on the ash blonde hair dye Moira was still holding. She pointed her pole at Moira. 'Does your mammy know you're thinking of becoming a bottle blonde?'

Moira shoved the box back on the shelf. 'I was just looking. Lovely to see you, Mrs Farrell. I hope you get that click sorted.' She and Andrea beat a hasty retreat and were headed out the automatic doors. They'd forgotten what they'd come for after the carry-on with Rosemary Farrell and Andrea only stopped when a meaty hand clamped down on her shoulder.

'Hold it right there, miss.'

Andrea spun round, wondering who it was accosting her.

A burly security guard dropped his hand as he stood over her and said, 'I'd like you to open your bag, please.'

Andrea's gaze flew to Moira stricken as she said, 'I forgot to pay.'

'Jaysus wept, Andrea.'

'I hid it in my bag, didn't I, so your clicky hip woman wouldn't see it and ask questions.' She was speaking rapidly as panic set in.

Moira looked at the security guard's badge and said, 'Whoa there, Ned.' In the same tone you might a frisky pony, then batting her lashes and putting on a breathy Marilyn Monroe sort of a voice, albeit with a Dublin accent, purred, 'There's been a misunderstanding. That's all, it's easily explained.'

Ned frowned, his eyes disappearing underneath two hungry caterpillar eyebrows. Your Demi Moore one could turn on the charm offensive all she liked. It wouldn't wash with him.

He'd not have his head turned by a pretty face. He was a trained crime-fighting professional, so he was.

'Well then, if your friend here opens her bag and there's nothing in there that shouldn't be in there we can get this all cleared up, can't we? And youse can both be on your way.'

'And would we get an apology, too, for the manhandling like?' Moira asked.

'Shut up, Moira.' Andrea glared at her before fixing her attention on the guard. 'The thing is, Ned, there *is* something in there. Only, I didn't mean to walk out without paying for it. I forgot that's all. How about I just go and pay for it now?' She made to move away but Ned blocked her way, placing his hand on her shoulder once more.

Moira thought he looked very much like he was dying to say, 'You're nicked,' like on that old television show her daddy had liked, *The Sweeney*.

'Listen, miss, we can do this the hard way or we can do it the easy way. It's up to you but I'll not ask you again. Open your bag.'

Andrea's bottom lip trembled as she unzipped her handbag and held it open.

Ned plucked the test kit out from where it sat on top of her makeup bag and purse and held it aloft like he was raising the Olympic torch.

'I'm not a shoplifter,' Andrea sniffed.

'She's not a shoplifter,' Moira affirmed. 'Don't worry, I won't let you go down for this, Andrea. We're in this together.'

Andrea looked at Ned as tears welled in her cocoa-coloured eyes, 'It's not even for me. It's for her.' She pointed a trembling finger at Moira.

So much for united we stand, Moira thought, as Ned ordered them to follow him upstairs while they got this matter sorted.

It was then Moira and Andrea became aware of all the pairs of eyes staring accusingly at them as they watched the unfolding action happening at the front of the shop.

Moira wondered if she could hold her jacket up over her face like celebrities coming out of court do and then realised it was too late to worry about being spotted. There, at the front of the checkout queue, was Rosemary Farrell and standing behind her with a can of shaving foam and packet of razors was Andrea's number one crush, Connor Reid.

Chapter Three

An hour and a half had passed by the time Andrea and Moira were told they were free to leave Boots, once they'd paid for the test that was. They'd been sat like naughty children in the principal's office for the duration of that time. Ned had frogmarched them up the stairs to the store manager's office where they'd had to wait until the lunchtime rush was over before she joined them.

They'd opted, after much conferring and red-faced urging that justice be handed down on Ned's part, not to ring the gards for which both girls were grateful. Moira suspected though if Ned had been left to decide their fate he'd have had them both in stocks in the village square. He'd have probably been selling the rotten tomatoes to biff at them too.

The store manager, however, who, despite her resemblance to Margaret Thatcher with too much makeup on, had a soft heart and an apparent dislike for Ned. She opted to take their story at face value. As such, they were let off with a warning not to try and leave the store with unpaid-for items stashed in their handbags in the future.

Moira had elbowed Andrea to shut up and nod along as she opened her mouth to protest that she hadn't intended to leave without paying for the tenth time.

'How am I going to live this down?' Andrea asked, now glaring at Ned before she strode towards the freedom on the other side of those automatic doors. Moira didn't answer, only pausing to pay for the pregnancy test. Once she'd stashed it out of sight and had the receipt in her hot little hand she went outside to join her friend.

The foot traffic had dissipated now and both girls stood there gulping in the sweet taste of liberty.

'Rosemary Farrell will be burning up the telephone line to Mammy as we speak. If she hasn't already called around in person to convey the news her daughter and friend were collared for nicking a pregnancy test kit that is.' Moira winced imagining her mammy's reaction. She was very glad Mammy didn't own a hiking pole.

'I didn't nick it.' Andrea was indignant and then, glancing at her watch said 'Sweet Jaysus, would you look at the time! It's after three o'clock. Nora will be going mad. She's a demon on Friday afternoons. Everything's urgent and has to be done before the close of business as if Monday won't roll around and the end of the world is nigh.' She hesitated and looked close to tears. 'They'll all know what happened. Why did it have to be Connor Reid of all people who was waiting in the checkout queue? Why? Now he'll think I'm pregnant *and* a shoplifter. He's bound to have mentioned it to his secretary and mealy-mouthed Melva will be burning up the internal lines. I won't be known as Nora McManus's poor secretary. I'll be known as the girl in the taxation department who pinched a pregnancy test kit from Boots. I'm mortified so I am.'

'I'm so sorry, Andrea.' Moira despite having told Andrea it was a weird habit, was doing the clenching of the bottom herself. 'We should stick together.' Mind you, she wasn't holding her breath given how quick her pal had been to point the finger at her when the going got rough. 'Come up with a good story. You know something like it was all a big misunderstanding and we were being secret squirrels with the test because it's for a friend whose identity we can't reveal.'

'I suppose.' Andrea didn't look convinced. 'Even if it does sound like a plot for one of the Shirley Conran books my mam's always got her head in and, Moira, if anyone so much as glances at my tummy I shall be telling them the truth.'

Moira couldn't say much to that. She'd do the same.

'Are you going back to college?'

'No, there's no point now. I'd be finishing at four anyway. Aisling's on a Viking tour, checking it out for guests as we speak so I'm going to go home and put myself out of my misery.' She tapped her bag.

Andrea forgot she was annoyed. 'I wish I could come with you but I'd best get back to work. Will you phone me as soon as you know?'

Moira nodded. It was the least she could do given what they'd gone through to get the test.

'It'll be alright.' Andrea gave her a hug. 'Ring me,' she said before hurrying off in the opposite direction to face the music at Mason Price while Moira dragged her heels all the way back to O'Mara's.

BRONAGH'S EYES PEERED furtively over the top of the desk as the door opened.

'It's alright, Bronagh, it's only me. Don't choke on your biscuit,' Moira said closing the door behind her.

The guesthouse's receptionist finished chomping and swallowed, brushing the telltale crumbs off her skirt. 'You're back early, Moira. Good day was it?'

Moira couldn't bring herself to go that far. 'It was alright.' She didn't hang about to chat. Bronagh was like Mammy. She'd the sixth sense when it came to knowing when she, Aisling or Rosi were up to something and she wasn't in the mood for the Spanish inquisition, not after the afternoon she'd had.

'I'm starving, Bronagh,' She wasn't hungry despite not having had lunch but the need for food pronto was something Bronagh understood and as such she was excused without further ado.

She took to the stairs, hearing the rustle of the biscuit packet which meant the receptionist was helping herself to another. Under normal circumstances, as Bronagh's former personal trainer, she'd tell her to put it back but today she didn't care whether she snaffled the whole packet.

Reaching the first-floor landing, Moira spied Idle Ita living up to her nickname. She'd her back to her and was so engrossed in the game she was playing on her phone that she didn't look back to see who it was. She'd been in the process of vacuuming the hall outside the guests' rooms when the urgent need to bring up Snake on her Nokia had overcome her. The vacuum cleaner was forgotten on the floor beside her.

'Don't work too hard there, Ita. I wouldn't want you to get the back strain or anything,' Moira couldn't resist calling out. Aisling was far too soft on her but Moira wasn't frightened to give her a nudge.

Ita jumped and the phone disappeared back in her pocket lickety-split. 'How're you, Moira? My poor mammy's under the weather and I was just texting her to see if she wanted me to pick up anything for her on my way home.'

Moira half expected their self-titled director of housekeeping's nose to grow as the fib tripped off her tongue. She doubted very much whether Ita's mam even had a mobile phone. If her mam wasn't an old friend of their mammy's she wouldn't still be here but there'd be murder if she was let go.

'Oh dear. I hope she feels better soon. Aisling will be back any minute,' Moira added pointedly.

At the thought of the boss putting in an appearance, Ita gunned the hoover and Moira carried on her way. The guesthouse was quiet this time of day with no sign of life on the next floor. Most of the guests wouldn't be back from their Dublin adventures until later that afternoon when they returned with the intention of relaxing for a while before heading out to dinner.

The apartment, when Moira pushed the door open, was silent and she took a deep breath. There was no point putting it off any longer. Tossing her jacket over a chair, she dumped her bag on the dining table before fishing out the box that had already caused them so much trouble.

'Here goes,' she muttered to the empty room, traipsing off to the bathroom.

FIVE MINUTES LATER, Moira sat on the toilet seat with the lid down and stared at the stick in her hand. There were two vivid pink lines glaring back at her. It hadn't changed when she'd closed her eyes and counted to ten before reopening them. She did it again just to be sure. *Definitely two lines.*

She got up and put the stick down on the bathroom vanity before peering into the mirror. She half expected to see herself changed. That a sensible, grown-up version of her would gaze back at her. Instead, she saw a pale, frightened girl as she said to her reflection, 'You, Moira O'Mara are going to be a mammy.'

Chapter Four

Downstairs, Bronagh was crumpling the empty packet of custard creams up, oblivious as she tossed them in the bin to the drama unfolding upstairs for the youngest O'Mara child.

She looked at the packet lying alongside the scrunched-up paper of processed bookings and plastic wrap from her lunchtime sandwiches. It was like saying goodbye to an old friend, she thought. Then, turning her attention to the crumbs on the desk she swept them into the palm of her hand and emptied them in the bin too.

Bronagh stood up and tilted her head from side to side. She'd a crick in her neck from having been hunched over the keyboard loading a tour group from Canada's faxed booking. She gave it a gentle rub. Nina would be here in a few minutes to take over for the evening shift and her eyes swept the reception area to ensure it was spick and span. She liked to leave her workspace tidy and expected to find it as she'd left it in the morning.

Bronagh slid into her jacket. A shoulder-padded number in a lovely autumnal burnt orange to mark the changing season. She'd been delighted this morning as she breezed along the street towards the guesthouse to notice the leaves had begun to turn across the road in the Green. Autumn with its crisp air and crunch of leaves beneath the feet was her favourite season.

Her shopping list was folded in her jacket pocket and, retrieving it, she jotted down custard creams. She'd stop at the butcher's on the way home too and get some of Neville's tasty pork sausages for her and her mam's dinner. They usually enjoyed bangers and mash once a week. She'd half a cabbage in the fridge needing using too. Pork sausages with potatoes and cabbage. Her mouth watered at the very thought.

The notion of custard creams and pork sausages saw her glance down at her skirt which was riding up. She tugged it back down. It was a respectable knee length that matched her jacket but was in danger of becoming a micro mini if she kept expanding the way she was.

She'd done so well losing weight for Aisling's wedding and it hadn't been easy. Moira, her self-appointed personal trainer, had had her running up and down those stairs as if she were trialling for Ireland's steeplechase. That was months ago now and so much had happened. She'd long since piled the pounds back on.

Bronagh's problem was she was a happy eater. She also reached for the sweet treats when she was in a low mood or a bad mood or wound up. But she munched even more when she was in fine fettle and she was in very fine fettle indeed these days.

Oh, she was sure if a psychiatrist were to venture their opinion they'd say she was addicted to the endorphins released when she nibbled on a custard cream. And she was sure they'd be right too. There were worse things to be hooked on in life though.

Leonard Walsh was the man responsible for the tightness of her skirt. Lenny as she fondly called him these days and the menopause, of course, not that the latter made her happy. It was a scourge upon a woman's figure and wellbeing that was.

At an age, however, when she'd thought herself long past love and with a future of hot flushes and the caring of her poor mammy stretching long, she'd fallen head over heels with the guesthouse regular who travelled across the water from Liverpool to visit his sister here in Dublin.

It was a wonderous thing life with its unexpected twists and turns, Bronagh thought happily instantly wanting to eat a biscuit.

Lenny's visits back to Dublin where he'd grown up were becoming more frequent and Bronagh relished their time together. He'd a penchant for the sweet things in life too and when he came to stay they were always sure to visit their favourite bakery, Cherry on Top, to see what their latest cake offerings were.

It worried her that he left Bessie, his dog, more and more with Harry his bowling pal. She'd like to meet Bessie; she felt as though she knew the dog well. It would be a lovely thing indeed to take Bessie for a walk together and to pause now and again to admire the glorious colours in the leafy canopy overhead. Perhaps Bessie and Pooh would become friends given the chance. Yes, this business of living in separate countries was a complicated one.

She'd yet to meet Leonard's sister, Joan, either and she only lived a half-hour walk away from the guesthouse. This wasn't sitting right with Bronagh. She'd broached the subject of an introduction to Joan more than once with Leonard but he'd been maddeningly evasive. She'd let it go but it was niggling at her. It was high time she met the remaining member of his family and stepped inside what had been his childhood home where Joan still resided.

It was O'Mara's proximity to his sister and the house in which he'd grown up that had initially seen Leonard book in with them. He wouldn't stay with Joan despite it sounding as though there were loads of room, claiming they got on grand so long as they weren't under the same roof.

This attitude puzzled Bronagh because the house had been his home too and he'd every right to stay there on his trips to Dublin. His parents, he'd confided, had left it to both their children in equal shares. Joan was happy there and he was content to leave things as they were.

She supposed too if he'd opted to sleep in his old room on his visits to their Fair City they'd never have met.

She'd like to visit the house where Leonard grew up to get a sense of what he was like as a lad. His sister, she knew, like her, had never married. They had that in common. She'd cared for hers and Leonard's father when his health failed as well. So, they'd that in common too. Bronagh felt she and Joan would get along just fine given the opportunity. She'd very much enjoy sitting down for a cosy chat with her to hear all about what Lenny was like as a lad.

Bronagh moved over to the sofa near the entrance and plumped the cushions with a sigh. These were the only blips on her blissful horizon. Time was marching on and she was beginning to wonder if she and Lenny would continue as they were with snatched visits here and there. Or, whether they'd take the next step as Maureen was doing with Donal and come to a permanent arrangement.

She knew which she'd prefer. She'd very much like to take the next step but it hovered over that frightening abyss of change. One of them was going to have to make big changes if they were to move forward with their relationship.

Was she prepared to move to Liverpool? She'd never even been to the city across the water. Then there was her mam. She'd have to come with her, obviously, if she were to make the move. Would it be fair to take her away from the only place she'd ever called home?

There was no question of her sister stepping up and doing her bit. The care of their poorly mam would fall on Bronagh as it had always done. She didn't mind. It was the way it was. She'd long since accepted her role. Besides, she loved her mam dearly and couldn't imagine not having her there of an evening to chat about her day with.

Lenny got on very well with her too. He liked her and she liked him and in that respect, Bronagh was blessed.

Of course, it would be much easier all around if Lenny were to move back to Dublin. She couldn't make that decision for him though. It was up to him and either way one of them would be leaving the familiar daily routines of their lives behind.

The door opened then, distracting Bronagh from her thoughts. The rumble of traffic filtered into the quiet of the reception area and Nina stamped her feet on the mat before bending to pick up the yellow leaf she'd brought in with her.

'Bello,' she murmured with a look on her face Bronagh couldn't work out.

'Hello there, Nina,' she said, packing her thoughts away as she went to retrieve her bag. She'd pork sausages to be buying. 'Have you had a good day?'

'Si, gracias, Bronagh.'

She looked well, Bronagh thought, giving the pretty Spanish girl the once over. She'd been worried about their young night concierge. She'd been quiet, almost withdrawn of late but this afternoon she seemed more her bubbly self.

'I had a letter from home.'

Ah, so that was it. She'd been homesick, Bronagh twigged. 'And is your family well?'

Nina nodded her face dimpling, 'They are buena.'

Bronagh nodded, 'Good, that's very good. I'll be off now then.'

'Adios, Bronagh.'

As Bronagh set off down the street her thoughts turned to Lenny's sister once more. There was no reason she couldn't call around and introduce herself. He was bound to have mentioned her to his sister.

Perhaps Joan thought it peculiar she hadn't knocked on her door? Men had no idea about things like that. Her mammy had a saying that always made her smile. 'They're as thick as manure, Bronagh, and only half as useful,' she'd say.

Yes, she resolved. One of these afternoons she'd pick a treat up from Cherry on Top and take it around because if Joan was anything like her brother, a slice of cake was sure to win her over.

Chapter Five

Joan

Joan Walsh felt a spark of excitement as she homed in on the Toby jug sat on the busy shelf. It was tucked away alongside a shepherdess figurine, a willow-patterned teacup and saucer, and a set of clover embossed salt and pepper shakers.

She was oblivious to the musty smell of the thrift shop or the odour of cigarettes radiating off the man pawing through the records in the box on the floor. A young girl clad in an outlandish fifties dress murmured excuse me as she brushed past her but Joan barely registered her so intent was she on examining the treasure she'd found.

She plucked it from the shelf and turned it upside down. It was fairly priced she decided, inspecting the white sticker. She looked at the porcelain, rosy-cheeked woman with her shiny black hair depicted and almost said hello to her.

She'd be a character, Joan mused, feeling the weight of the jug in her hand. A woman who'd be called Mollie or Annie, or something like that. She'd like to bake bread, make apple pies, sing songs and would be the sorta woman who'd be inclined to spread tittle-tattle about the village, she decided.

That was what Joan liked about these jugs. She knew right enough some thought the ceramics ugly but she saw more than a leering porcelain mug. She created personalities for them. They felt like friends. She'd quite the collection at the home.

'Goodness, that's a face you wouldn't forget in a hurry,' a woman with silver hair which was cut short and had the sort of natural curl Joan had coveted when she was younger.

'I think she looks like an Annie or a Mollie, what do you think?' Joan said smiling.

The woman's eyes danced and she smiled back. 'Definitely an Annie.'

They whiled away five minutes chatting about the different treasures they'd unearthed from the various St Vincent de Paul and Age Concern shops around town.

And there it was in a nutshell—what Joan, a lonely woman, enjoyed about her Toby jugs because bawdy they might be but they were also conversation starters. They broke the ice with strangers and gave her something to talk about with a likeminded individual.

Joan had been painfully shy as a child. She'd had Brigid, her best friend. They'd been thick of thieves through their childhood and on into their teenage years until the night of the circus when everything changed.

She'd gone on to college and then into the workforce and she'd blossomed a little, making new friends, but eventually, those friends had married and started families. She'd fallen by the wayside because they wanted friends with whom they could chat in earnest about nappies, teething, and sleepless nights. All of which Joan had no clue about.

To Joan's mind parenthood sounded a terrible business and she was happy to stick with her collections. Nobody had seen her collections as a problem back then and she much preferred her inanimate treasures because they didn't cry, poop, and demand. They were solid and reliable in a world Joan had discovered that long-ago night when everything had changed irrevocably, was anything but.

Now, she said cheerio to the woman, who moved on to inspect the glassware, and took her latest acquisition to the counter.

'Another jug is it, Joan? I wondered if you'd spot her.' Nuala who volunteered in the shop on a Friday knew Joan's shopping habits well. 'I don't know where you find the room to put all the bric-a-brac you cart home.' She rang the ceramic up and took Joan's money before wrapping it in newspaper and popping it in a bag for her.

Joan didn't smile because therein lay her problem. She'd run out of room a long time ago but it hadn't stopped her collecting more and more. 'Ah, I can always move a few things about. Sure, one small jug, it'll be grand. Thank you, Nuala.'

'See you next week, Joan.'

Joan walked past the odorous man who was examining an album, and out the door which jingled as she opened it. She closed it behind her and glanced down the row of shops. She'd no need to stop anywhere else today. She was eager to get Annie home and find a place for her to live.

Her back was giving her bother today and she winced at the sudden pinch as she moved past the butchers and the Spar onto the suburban stretch of the road that would lead her towards her house.

Age was letting itself be known in the form of sneaky aches and pains. She'd have liked to have walked at a faster pace. She'd never been one to drag her heels but she'd no choice now and she was soon meandering past the familiar brick houses she'd been walking past for most of her life.

Had she really once skipped along this pavement? She shook her head at the memory of the girl she'd been. The young never think age will catch them.

'Hello there, Mary. It's a beautiful day, isn't it?' Joan was glad to come to a halt. The day was unseasonably warm as though summer had decided to give it one last hurrah.

Mary McNulty was kneeling on a cushion in her front garden. She peered up from under her wide-brimmed straw hat, secateurs in hand. 'It's grand, Joan. It's time to cut back for winter. Not that you'd believe it's around the corner on a day like today.' She waved her secateurs over the trimmed-back hydrangeas. 'I'm hoping for a good show from my hydrangeas next summer.'

'Your front garden always looks a treat, Mary.'

Mary smiled; she loved her garden. She liked to sit in her front room with the chair angled just so and catch the admiring glances of passers-by as the brilliant pinks, purples and blues of her favourite bushes caught their eye. It was her reward for her hard work.

'And how are you keeping, Joan?' A funny woman was Joan Walsh. Secretive and hermit-like in that house which was far too big for one. She took in the woman's old-fashioned blouse and skirt. Her slate coloured hair was knotted back in a prim bun. A dowdy sight indeed, Mary thought. They were around the same age but she still coloured her hair and planned on doing so a good while longer yet.

Joan's garden was the stuff of Mary's nightmares. It was in dire need of a weed and cutting back. It was a scourge on an otherwise attractive neighbourhood and she was glad she'd no thoughts of selling because Joan's place would surely lower the prices of all the others on the street.

She wondered what the house was like inside. Joan didn't strike her as the house-proud sort. That brother of hers who came to visit from time to time needed to take her in hand, she mused, all the while smiling up at her.

'I'm well, thank you, Mary. I'd best be on my way now. I look forward to seeing your hydrangeas next summer.' Joan was about to carry on her way when Mary, spotting the plastic bag with the newspaper-wrapped jug, asked. 'What have you bought today then?'

'A Toby jug, she's a beauty.' Joan's face lit up.

'A Toby jug,' Mary echoed. 'I couldn't be doing with one of them grinning down at me from the sideboard. No, I'm a Wedgewood woman me.'

'Each to their own, Mary,' Joan said setting off, not in the least offended. She'd the measure of Mary McNulty. Joan was a good judge of character and she'd no wish to exchange anything other than brief pleasantries with the woman. In days gone by, she'd have been fitted with a scold's bridle!

It was Gordon she came across next on her familiar route. Like her, he was a creature of habit, or had been since he'd lost his wife a few years ago. Joan hadn't known her well but what she had known of her, she'd liked. She'd seemed a kind woman with a good heart.

Gordon was lonely and, as Joan knew how this felt, she'd begun to look forward to their chats.

'How're you, Joan?' He gave her a wave from where he was sitting on the park bench. The seat was on the grassy verge of the reserve the council was forever making noises about putting houses on but never seemed to get around to doing so.

The day's newspaper was open in front of him and he peered overtop before folding it closed.

'Very well, Gordon. How's yourself? Enjoying the glorious sunshine, I see.'

'I am indeed, Joan, and I can't complain. Why don't you join me and show me what you're after buying today?'

She sat down next to him and fished her newspaper parcel out, unwrapping it carefully to show him. She let him take it from her.

'My, my, she strikes me as the sort who'd have a lot to say for herself.' Gordon's eyes twinkled as he turned the jug over in his hands. 'A bit like her down the road doing her garden.'

Joan's mouth twitched at the reference to Mary McNulty. 'I think you might be right there. What do you think, Gordon, is she an Annie or a Molly? Or, perhaps a Mary?' She cast a side-long glance at him and saw his mouth twitch at her comeback.

'Hmm, I'd say an Annie.'

'Well now, seeing as you're the second person to say that Annie it is.' Joan dimpled taking the jug back and re-wrapping it before slipping it back in the bag. She did enjoy their Friday banter.

'So, what's been happening in the world today then?'

Gordon rustled his paper. 'Would you believe, they've only managed to implant an artificial heart in a chap over in America. Imagine that,' his hand went to his chest.

'Tis a wonder what the doctors can do nowadays,' Joan said as if she were a fountain of knowledge on medical breakthroughs. 'There'll come a time when they'll be able to grow all our bits and pieces from our own cells; mark my words it'll happen, Gordon.'

'I don't doubt you, Joan. But I don't know if it's a good thing or not. It's murky waters this living longer business.'

They whiled away half an hour lamenting the state of the world after that and putting it to rights before Joan stood up once more. She gave him a cheery wave goodbye and went on her way. She wondered if Gordon's afternoon loomed as long as hers did.

She was red in the face from the unexpected heat of the day by the time she put her key in the front door. She unlocked it and pushed open the door with its peeling green paint until the gap was wide enough for her to slip through. She closed it behind her and peered up the gloom of her hallway. The overflowing boxes stacked in a haphazard manner had had Leonard stewing on his last visit because he thought them unsafe. He said the whole lot would come down on her one of these days.

She did feel bad that he refused to stay here with her. It had been his home too, once upon a time. She'd offered to clear some space but he'd not hear of it and had settled into the habit of staying at that guesthouse by St Stephen's Green. This had worked out well for him by all accounts because he had a new lease on life since he'd begun courting the woman who worked on the hotel's front desk. Bronagh her name was.

Joan would like to meet her but she knew Leonard wouldn't invite her here and as yet there'd been no mention of Joan joining them elsewhere.

Leonard was ashamed of her. She knew that. She was his guilty secret. She didn't want it to be that way but she didn't know how to change either.

She shook the upsetting thoughts of her brother away and focused on her treasure instead, and squeezing around the corner into the front room she gazed about her pondering where Annie should go.

The net curtains afforded her privacy but allowed sunlight to dapple over her things. This had always been her mam's favourite room. Her mam had had the most beautiful Noritake china dinner service set. It had been housed in the sideboard. The original unit was long gone but Joan had its replacement wedged up against the wall.

As a child, Joan would sit on the floor with the doors to the cabinet open where she was allowed to look but not touch her mam and dad's beautiful wedding present. She'd gaze at the delicate floral patterns and gold edgings of the plates and bowls in wonder that anybody could produce something so delicate.

'I'd like to go to Japan one day, Mam. I want to visit the village where this was made.' Her mam had told her the story that the china had come from a small village, with the Name of Noritake and that it had been shipped to Ireland by entrepreneurial American brothers.

'Good for you, Joanie,' Mam would smile over the rim of her teacup.

Of course, she'd never gone to Japan and never would now either, she suspected, retrieving the jug and unwrapping it for the last time.

'You're home now,' she said to Annie, knowing she'd a busy afternoon ahead of her deciding where on earth this latest treasure of hers was to go.

Chapter Six

Joan

Joan shuffled the pile of old Christmas cards and letters aside and put her tea down on the kitchen table. She pulled her chair out and sat down, cocooned in the space filled with things she'd accumulated over her lifetime. Things she couldn't let go of. Some treasures and some not so much, she thought, flicking a glance at the rubbish bags piling up by the door.

She knew exactly when her collecting had begun. Her fascination with beautiful, unusual, and downright quirky objects had ignited as she gazed at her mam's china set when she was small but her first foray into the art of collection had begun with stamps.

She'd been given the teal, leather-bound book with the words My First Stamp Album embossed in gold on the cover when she turned ten. It had special acid free pages and little strips for pinioning the stamps to them. Joan had ripped the pretty wrapping paper off and sitting there cross-legged on the floor admiring it, she'd thought it the best present she'd ever received.

There was a one-cent stamp from America already affixed to the first page inside. It was green and had the Statue of Liberty on it. Her mammy's friend Ann, who'd emigrated with her family to Boston a few years earlier, wrote to her regularly and mam had saved it for her.

Her mam's lovely swirly inked inscription wishing her a happy tenth birthday from mammy, Daddy, and Leonard decorated the inside cover.

Even now, Joan could recall the thrill of steaming a particularly eye-catching stamp off an envelope for her album. She'd insisted her mam spread the word amongst her friends that they were to save their envelopes for Joan's inspection before they were screwed up and tossed on the fire, just in case there was a stamp worth keeping amidst them.

She'd kept the album in the drawer of her bedside table and by the time she'd gotten it out shyly to show her new friend, Brigid, she'd half the pages filled.

Brigid had come home with her after school. Joan could recall how proud she'd felt sailing out the school gates with her. She was a very pretty girl with startling blue eyes and raven hair and Joan had hoped some of her allure would rub off on her. Brigid's large family had recently moved from Galway to Dublin and everyone wanted to be the new girl's friend.

Brigid had been particularly enamoured with Joan's pride and joy, a red-edged stamp with a majestic stag standing stock still in waving grass as it stared at something in the distance only it could see. Hills rolled in the background and the stag was shaded by a leafy tree. It was more an artwork than a stamp and had been sent to her by her French pen pal, Estelle.

Joan had been beside herself with excitement when she'd seen it and she'd swiftly found herself pen pals in Italy and Sweden too. She'd been a busy girl thanks to her stamp collecting.

She'd thought she'd visit the places her stamps originated from one day. She'd be brave like that Joan of Arc they'd learned about in a history lesson recently. But then, just like Joan, her dreams had gone up in flames.

It was Brigid who'd set the wheels in motion for her need to collect, she supposed, looking back now. In more ways than one.

She'd gone to school the next day and told the other girls about Joan's beautiful stamp all the way from France. Word had spread and an after-school invitation to Joan Walsh's house to see the coveted stamp had become a sought-after commodity.

Joan enjoyed telling her peers she was interested in philately too. The flicker of interest at the mention of such an unusual word from her parents' friends didn't escape her notice. It made her feel special and inevitably led to her producing her album.

The shy girl who'd always preferred to listen rather than speak could chat for hours about her stamps. They'd opened up a world of conversation for her.

Stamps allowed the ordinary child with the slightly crossed front teeth and mouse-brown hair to become interesting. It didn't matter if she wasn't beautiful like Brigid because to be interesting was just as good, better even.

She'd even thought she might like to become a philatelist if it were possible but then the fire had ripped through their home and everything had changed. Most of all, she'd changed.

Joan sipped her tea and remembered.

1945

Joan's satchel rubbed at her uniform causing it to pill in a manner that had her mam tutting as she scuffed her feet along the pavement. One sock had pooled around her ankle and the other was threatening to join it. She didn't stop to pull them up.

She wasn't in good form because she'd have liked to have Brigid come home with her today but Mammy had said she wasn't to invite anyone back to the house because she wouldn't be there. It was Aunt Terri's birthday and her mam was meeting her in the city for a posh lunch and a day's shopping. It was tradition, she'd said, as she'd applied her lipstick.

Joan had been fascinated watching the slick of red stain her mam's lips. She'd been even more captivated as she applied two dots of the red to her cheek and rubbed them in with her fingertips. 'Go on now, Joan, or you'll be late,' Mammy had said, fluffing with her hair.

It wasn't an option for her to go to Brigid's house. She'd never been there and this bothered Joan. She'd have liked to have seen where her best friend and the horde of brothers and sisters she had lived.

Joan had a natural curiosity about her and she liked to catch glimpses of other people's lives. Brigid was always coy though when she hinted as to the possibility of going to her house after school for a change. She'd say it was much nicer going to the peace and quiet of Joan's house and sure, who'd be bothered with all her brothers and sisters listening in on their conversation anyway?

She'd mentioned Brigid's reluctance to invite her home to her mammy and she'd said perhaps she had her reasons. As such, if Joan wanted to remain friends with her, she needed to respect them. It had been an unsatisfactory answer in Joan's opinion because how could she respect what she didn't understand? It also made her feel her mam knew something she didn't about Brigid's family.

The distant sound of jingling bells signalling an emergency of some sort distracted her and she wondered what it was. As she trudged on, the acrid smell of smoke caught in the back of her throat. Joan coughed and her eyes smarted.

There was a fire she surmised, picking up her pace and wondering where it was. She carried on towards home, unintentionally following the sound of the bells and the smell of burning.

By the time she reached her road, Joan's eyes were beginning to stream and she could see a crowd of people gathered on the street, all looking towards the house with black smoke billowing from it. Scarlet flames leapt out of the living room window.

Joan was frozen to the spot, not believing what she was seeing. It was as if the fire were eating everything it could reach. Two fire trucks swished water in through the windows of her home and then, without even being aware of it she was running towards those hungry flames.

'Stop, Joan!' Leonard caught hold of her, his grasp on her shoulders firm outside their front gate as he pulled her to a stop.

'Mammy? Daddy?' she choked out, her eyes wild as she looked at the hollow space of their front room.

'There's nobody in there, Joanie. It's alright,' her brother soothed but she could hear the tremor in his voice. He'd been frightened too, she realised. 'Mrs O'Malley across the way has rung Dad at work and told him what's happening. Mam's in town, remember? She's not back as yet.'

Joan was grateful for that but Leonard was wrong; it was far, far from alright.

When at last the fire, which had done considerable damage to the hall, kitchen, and front room but hadn't licked its way up the stairs was doused, they'd picked about the waterlogged, charred rooms to see what could be salvaged.

Her mam's beautiful Noritake china lay shattered in mosaic pieces and Joan's precious stamp album that she'd had out just the night before to show her dad her latest acquisition all the way from Zimbabwe, thanks to her Swedish friend having an uncle there, was no more than a heap of ashes. Why hadn't she put it away? Why'd she left it, forgotten about, on the table beside her dad's chair? If she'd taken it upstairs with her she'd still have it.

They'd gone to stay with family, crowding into their front room until their own home was repaired. After a while, the others forgot they'd lost nearly everything. Joan, however, hadn't been able to understand how you could leave home and everything was normal and return to find nothing the same. She'd become withdrawn and nervy. And she couldn't get the smell of smoke from nostrils.

Mammy, concerned by her ongoing anxiousness where the fire was concerned had explained that they were fortunate because things could be replaced but people couldn't. Joan knew this wasn't true because she couldn't replace the feelings her beautiful album had conjured. They were gone for good. Burned to a crisp.

Now Joan drained her cup and got up from her seat. She left her tea things on the table because there was no room in the sink. She'd sort it later. The window sill above the sink however was clear. Nothing was ever displayed there because that was how the fire had started. Not, as she'd suspected from one of her dad's cigarettes which he was apt to leave smouldering in the ashtray. They'd found this out once the firemen had packed their hoses away.

Mam had always loved the way the low-lying winter sun streamed in through the kitchen windows that overlooked the back garden. The day of the fire it had shone in through the glass vase she'd washed and dried before placing it on the sill where it wouldn't get accidentally knocked over. It had acted as a magnifier and the cloth on the kitchen table had begun to smoke before igniting.

This was why the window sill was the only place in the entire house where there was nothing on display.

Chapter Seven

'Moira, it's me, your mammy.'

Moira rolled her eyes. For feck's sake, she'd known the woman since she was born and that aside she'd known who it would be before she even picked up the telephone. She'd been expecting her call. The only surprise was it had taken Mammy this long to ring.

She'd been on tenterhooks since she'd arrived home from Boots expecting her to barge through the door of the family apartment once Rosemary Farrell had had the chance to relay what she'd seen play out that afternoon.

'Yes, I know who it is, Mammy.' Her eyes flitted over to Aisling who'd been back half an hour. She'd settled straight into a pedicure. It was her go-to stress relief along with Snowballs, a bag of which her hand was stuffed inside right at this moment.

She'd informed Moira when she arrived home that she'd experienced a near-death moment on the Viking boat that afternoon. It had occurred when a big woman all but jumped into the poor excuse for a boat Aisling found herself in. The boat had nearly overturned.

It had been a relief, Moira thought, not that Aisling nearly wound up in the Liffey, but that she was preoccupied with the drama of her own afternoon. Now she was too interested in her toenails to notice her sister's stricken face.

Aisling was ensconced on the sofa with her feet resting on the coffee table as she waited for her freshly painted, coral surprise, toenails to dry. Some inane game show with lots of canned laughter was on the television. She flicked her gaze towards her sister and Moira put her hand over the receiver.

'It's just Mammy.'

'Tell her I'm out,' Aisling said, in no mood for the 'when am I going to be a nana' chat. She watched as Moira took herself off to her room, relieved she was going to be spared.

Ever since Aisling had announced to all and sundry when they'd arrived home from Los Angeles that she and Quinn were trying for a baby and as such, she wanted to be added to everyone's prayers, Mammy had been checking in regularly. She was beginning to regret opening her mouth, thinking perhaps she'd tempted fate by speaking too soon because try as they might, nothing was happening. It was very disheartening.

They'd been trying longer than she'd let any of them know because she'd set her mind to getting in the family way as soon as she'd gotten the wedding ring on her finger. If she were honest, she'd thought it would happen within that first month but it hadn't and then the months had ticked by until they'd gotten to autumn. It was very hard counting down the days of each month on tenterhooks only to be disappointed. Los Angeles had been the only respite from the baby-making journey and once she'd gotten home she'd stepped up the ante.

She'd sensed Quinn hadn't been in the mood to perform last night too. This was a worry. They were hardly an old married couple. She'd coerced him into it on the basis that it could be their lucky night. No man could keep up the frenetic bedroom schedule she'd had him on these last months for any great length of time though so it had better happen soon, she mused. Then, and only then he could have a break from the riding.

In the meantime, she'd keep an eye out for oysters. Tesco had sold out thanks to her. The stupid overpriced, crustaceans hadn't worked anyway because Quinn had not been happy she'd blown the tight budget he had them on with her bulk shellfish purchase. So much for being good for a man's virility; all they'd done for him was raise his stress levels.

In her bedroom, Moira felt sick as she listened to the heavy breathing hissing down the line. This conversation not going to be good she thought, bracing herself and kicking her bedroom door shut with the heel of her foot. Mammy only did the Darth Vader breathing when something bad was after happening.

She flopped down on her bed and, unable to stand it any longer, said, 'Would you stop the breathing and speak to me, Mammy.'

There were two more in and out breaths and then Maureen in a high-pitched voice that sounded dangerously close to the edge said, 'I'm after hearing something that's got my knickers in a knot just now.'

Moira was on the defence which automatically turned her into even more of a smart-arse than unusual, according to her sisters anyway. 'Well, buy a bigger size, Mammy, that's my advice. Then they won't get all knotty.'

'Moira O'Mara, I'm not in the mood! Rosemary Farrell has just left and she's after telling me she saw you and Andrea get arrested at the Boots and that's not the worst of it.'

Here it comes, Moira clenched her bottom for the second time that day and silently cursed Rosemary Farrell.

'The pair of you were caught in the act of thieving a pregnancy test no less. A child of mine making a holy show of herself.'

Moira didn't need to see her to know her mammy was crossing herself and if you were to put her actions to music, she'd look like she was doing the arm aerobics.

'There was no thieving involved. It was a misunderstanding, Mammy, that's all. It's all been cleared up and sure we're not even barred from the store. We're on good terms with your Boots people.'

Maureen wasn't listening. She wanted to get down to the nitty-gritty crux of the matter. 'Is she expecting then?'

'Who?'

The Darth Vader breathing started up again and Moira decided she'd pushed her luck far enough. However, she was not up for telling the truth either so found herself telling her mammy in an equally high-pitched voice. 'Andrea was buying the test for her friend at work, that's all.'

Maureen snorted and Pooh by her side looked at her in alarm. 'That old chestnut.'

'What do you mean?'

'You can't pull the wool over my eyes, Moira O'Mara. I read your Shirley Conran woman's book.'

'What are you on about, Mammy?' Moira stared at the ceiling, willing the conversation to be over. It was going worse than she'd thought it would.

'The one with the girls all keeping it a secret as to who the mammy of your one who uses the 'b' word is when she asks which one of them is her mammy.'

Moira's head spun as she tried to work out what her mammy had just said. There was no sense to it she thought, biting down on her bottom lip. It was no good pretending. Mammy would have to know the truth sometime.

The thing was, Moira had always been one for putting off the things she didn't want to do. She was one of life's procrastinators. And so, she remained silent.

'And does Andrea's poor mammy know her daughter's been fornicating without the roll-on rubber things?'

'Jaysus wept Mammy!' The clenching happened automatically upon hearing this. 'Condoms.'

'That's what I said.'

Nope, Moira had never been one to rip the plaster off in one fell swoop. She'd a feeling she'd be better off owning up now though because Mammy would get to the bottom of what was going on sooner or later. She wouldn't put it past her to telephone Andrea's mammy either to commiserate.

She winced at the thought of her asking poor Mrs Reilly if her daughter had told her she was going to be a grandmother. Her friendship with Andrea had been stretched thin this afternoon already, and as tempted as she was, she couldn't risk it reaching breaking point.

'Listen, Mammy, I've something to tell you. It might come as a shock to you so sit down if you're not already.'

Darth Vader was back.

Moira took a deep breath of her own. 'It's not Andrea who's expecting. It's me.'

'Holy God above tonight!' Darth Vader breathing ensued followed by, 'I'm going to have to call a family conference.'

Chapter Eight

Donal closed the apartment door behind him and waved a hand in greeting at Maureen before pocketing the keys. He'd stopped at Tesco's and gotten in some things for their dinner and his arms felt like they belonged to an orangutang after having carted the bags up from the car park under the building.

Apartment living wasn't for him in the long term he'd decided and he was looking forward to finding a forever home for him and Maureen. Right now though, he'd a chicken curry to think about cooking. This was when he realised Maureen was looking peaky and she was after repeating the same phrase over and over.

Normally, Maureen would have enjoyed the relaxed familiarity of Donal letting himself into her apartment, not this afternoon though. She was far too heartily engaged in another round of Holy God above tonight's to even notice his return and, she was in shock.

They'd planned a relaxed evening with no mention of the house hunting they were in the midst of because it was a draining business so it was trying to find the perfect love nest. There'd be no relaxing now though, Moira had seen to that.

Pooh's poodly ears were twitching. He hadn't moved from Maureen's side as he listened to the pitch of his mistress's voice with alarm. The last time she'd adopted a tone like that had been when he'd cocked a leg over Donal's shoes. Speaking of whom, he was so engrossed in watching his beloved he'd forgotten to growl at Donal.

Across town, Moira, still lying on her bed, was protesting, 'But I don't want a family conference. I haven't even had the chance to talk to Tom yet, Mammy. It's not any of Rosi's, Pat's, or Ash's business anyway. And don't you be telling anybody until I've told Tom. Do you hear me?'

'Don't you be 'do you hearing me', young lady. You're in no position to be giving out to me.' Maureen's face turned a blotchy pink. 'And will he be wanting to make an honest woman of you, do you think? Or will you be a poor single mammy, struggling to make ends meet?'

'I haven't had a chance to think about anything yet, Mammy. It's too soon.'

'You're only after having sorted yourself out. You can't be looking after a baby.'

Moira knew she'd nearly crashed and burned but she had sorted herself out just as Mammy had said. She'd given up drinking, she'd enrolled in art college and she'd met Tom. She'd finally gotten on a path that made her happy and now this had happened. But it wasn't the dark ages. Women juggled all sorts successfully these days.

'I'll make it work, Mammy.'

'Well, don't be thinking you can fob the poor wee baby off on me. I've Donal to think of not to mention my entrepreneurial sidelines.'

Moira had been thinking precisely that. Her mammy had scary, supernatural mind-reading powers.

Donal's eyes popped hearing all this. He'd only been gone a few hours having called around to his daughter Anna's to fix a dripping tap before stopping at the supermarket. Now he'd surmised from the one-sided conversation he'd just overheard, a drama involving one of Maureen's girls being pregnant out of wedlock was unfolding. That ruled Aisling out. It was either Roisin or Moira and his money was on Moira given the ashen face on his beloved.

Besides, Roisin already had Noah and would manage alright on her own. She was a self-sufficient soul, unlike Moira. He hovered in the living area unsure what to do.

'She's only gone and got herself pregnant,' Maureen said, not bothering to put her hand over the mouthpiece. 'Can you believe it? Not only that, Donal, she was arrested at the Boots for shoplifting a pregnancy test. I'm mortified. The O'Mara name has been dragged through the mud today, so it has.'

'Mammy, don't be telling Donal.'

'As my man friend, Donal is my rock. There's no secrets between us. And I'll tell you something else, Pooh's in shock too, so he is.' She'd have to put some country music on once she got off the phone to soothe him, Maureen thought, reaching down to pet him.

'Donal, I was not arrested. It was a misunderstanding!' Moira shouted as loud as she dared not wanting Aisling to come running.

For his part, Donal heard something about arrested and a misunderstanding. He shook his head and embarked on a round of charades which, despite the gravity of the conversation she was in the middle of with her youngest child, Maureen's competitive spirit couldn't ignore.

She followed his movements through narrowed eyes deciding he was pouring something. It was tricky because he hadn't given her any categories. Still, she was usually up for a challenge.

Donal, she decided a moment later, was a man of many talents but playing charades wasn't one of them.

'Do the sounds like, Donal,' she instructed, cocking her other ear in readiness.

Donal decided it would be quicker to just say his piece. 'Would you like a glass of wine, Maureen?'

'Oh, now I see what you were trying to do with that pouring business. I was thinking along the lines of *Last of the Summer Wine.* Yes, a large one, Donal, please. Do you hear that, Moira O'Mara? You're driving your mammy to drink so you are.'

He was right then, Donal thought, moving to the fridge to offload the bags. There was a cold, half-full bottle of white in the fridge but he was mighty glad he'd bought more on his supermarket run; he'd a feeling Maureen was going to need it.

'I don't know what your sisters are going to say. And there's Aisling trying her hardest night after night with poor Quinn whose tadpoles won't turn into a frog.'

Moira couldn't believe what she was hearing. 'Sperm, egg, baby, Mammy, there's nothing froggy about it.'

'I know how it's done thanks very much. I had four of you. Just because you're seeing a student doctor you think you know it all these days.' Maureen paused to take the wine Donal was holding out to her and gave him a grateful smile before slugging back a gulp.

Moira listened to her mammy swallowing her wine with a stab of guilt but then it wasn't as if she'd planned for this to happen. Obviously, Tom was responsible too but how was he going to take this news? She clenched again. They'd never once talked children. Babies and the like was something hazy in the future that older grown-up couples like Aisling and Quinn with mortgages and their lives all sorted did.

A baby didn't fit into the scheme of their plans. They didn't actually have any plans, now that she thought about it. Only that they'd move in together and they hadn't even managed that yet.

Moira jumped as her mammy said, 'I suggest you tell your Tom the result of his ridey without your rubber roll-on thingamabob as soon as you get off the phone to me.'

'Mammy, don't be talking about condoms in front of Donal and I will tell Tom, it's just it's not a good time right now. He's all sorts of exams and things on at the moment.'

Maureen roared, 'Moira O'Mara, you'll not be doing your ostrich bit. You're pregnant so you are. You've a baby in that tummy of yours whatever Tom has on and it's only going to grow.' A thought occurred to her. 'You're not thinking about a trip to England are you?'

Maureen prided herself on being a forward-thinking woman but she was also Catholic and she didn't know how she'd feel if Moira decided to terminate the pregnancy.

'No, Mammy. I'm not.' Would Tom want her to have an abortion? He was a doctor in the making, he could be very clinical about things. The very thought of it made her sad.

'She's going to have the baby, Donal.' Maureen flung over her shoulder to Donal who'd begun to chop an onion.

Donal nodded carrying on with his methodical chopping.

Another thought made itself known. 'And what about adoption?' Maureen knew there were loads of couples desperate for a little one but this was her grandchild they were talking about and she didn't want to share.

'No, Mammy, I want my baby.' Moira realised she'd made her mind up irrespective of what Tom wanted.

'Well, if I'm to be a nana again and your sisters aunts and your brother an uncle we need to have the family conference.'

Ah Jaysus, Moira thought, Mammy was like a dog with a bone. 'We can't because Rosi's not here and neither's Pat.' Score to me, Moira thought triumphantly.

'Sure, they can listen in on the telephone.'

Moira frowned. She was fighting a losing battle because whether she liked it or not, Mammy would be having her family powwow. This meant she'd no wiggle room where Tom was concerned, she'd have to tell him first chance she got. He was working at Quinn's tonight. She'd have a chat with him once he'd finished his shift.

'I'll tell Tom tonight, Mammy.'

'And what about your sisters?'

'I'll tell them tomorrow after I've spoken to Tom,' Moira said then fibbed, 'I've got to go. Tom's expecting me around his.'

'Moira,' Maureen said, the wine having smoothed her frayed edges. 'I'm sure you're frightened.'

Moira felt tears prickle. She'd never been more scared in her life. 'I am.' She blinked rapidly. 'What if I'm an awful mammy?'

'Why would you be?'

'I was never much cop at looking after my dolls. Sure, they all lost limbs and had terrible haircuts.'

'Listen to me, you're an O'Mara woman, you'll be grand and sure haven't you got me and your sisters to help you. We all love you, Moira, and we'll all love the little one too. You'll not be on your own.'

This was true, Moira thought, sniffing. 'Thanks, Mammy,' she said before hanging the phone up. 'I'll be grand,' she whispered to herself.

Chapter Nine

'Moira, my Helen of Troy! It is I, your Paris, son of the Trojan king.' Alasdair the maître d' of Quinn's bistro minced forth and took hold of her hand. He brushed the back of it with his lips before releasing it.

Moira shook her head. 'You're mad, Alasdair. Completely mad.' He must have been a right history buff at school too, she thought. It wasn't that long ago he'd been telling her he was Hemingway in a past life and she was, whoever Hemingway was, the woman he'd been married to. It all went over the top of her head. She'd not been one for history, the nuns could vouch for that. Actually, she'd not been one for much at school other than art although she'd had a real talent Sister Mary had said for distracting others.

'You're looking particularly lovely tonight, Ms O'Mara.'

She knew Alasdair wasn't discriminating with his compliments. He said this to all the women who frequented Quinn's. His theatrical charm was a drawcard to the bistro which was well and truly on the tourist trail with its cosy traditional atmosphere. It wouldn't have mattered if she'd worn her oldest pair of tracksuit bottoms, he'd still carry on like so, not that she was complaining. Anyway, as it happened she had made a special effort tonight.

She'd spent ages peering in the mirror doing her makeup and had worn a microscopic dress she knew Tom particularly liked, figuring she might as well while she still could. She'd felt as though she were putting on armour. The dress was hidden under her belted maroon trench coat. Aisling said the coat made her look like she was the entertainment at a stag do but Moira fancied it made her look mysterious as in who knew what she was wearing underneath it?

'Will we be graced with any other members of the O'Mara family or have you come to make eyes at your Tom?'

'I'll be making eyes at my Tom, thank you, Alasdair, and I haven't booked I'm afraid. Is there any chance you could squeeze me in somewhere?' She should have telephoned and asked him to reserve a table for her, especially given it was Friday night.

A cacophonous burst of laughter went up and her eyes swept the heaving restaurant for the culprit. She couldn't spot them but she did spy Tom who'd yet to see her.

He wasn't expecting her; they'd arranged to meet up at his once his shift was finished. She liked their lazy Saturday mornings at his place even if she did get the daggers from Malcolm. He'd stopped buying the shredded wheat too she'd noticed. He was after getting in some unpalatable bran stuff that gave her terrible wind which didn't make for a saucy Saturday morning.

Tom had his back to her as he took an order from a table near the stage where a band of short, hairy Irishmen were setting up.

Alasdair tracked her line of vision. 'Quinn assures me they're grand musicians and fair play they've drawn a full house. Personally, though, I prefer The Sullivans. Your Roisin's Shay's a fine fiddler so he is and I'm sure she'd agree.'

Moira studied his deadpan expression. Sometimes she didn't know when he was joking with her or not.

'Still,' he said with a dismissive flap of his hand, I suppose they can't all look like the lads from Boyzone or Westlife. Would you believe that lot up there are called the Fiddling Feehans?'

Moira choked back a giggle, half at the inappropriate name and half at the expression on Alasdair's face.

'If I were their manager, I'd have called them The Hobbits. A much better fit, don't you think?'

He was a tonic was Alasdair, Moira thought, unable to stop the giggle escaping as she realised the vocalist did indeed have a hobbitty look about him.

She'd been so edgy when she'd left the guesthouse, refusing to meet Aisling's eye as she raced out the door. She'd barely acknowledged Nina on the desk either. She'd have to apologise to her when she saw her next. She'd a lot on her mind though.

'Come with me,' Alasdair ordered now, sashaying as only Alasdair could toward a table tucked away in the corner right by the toilets. 'We keep this table free for emergencies like botched bookings.'

Or people with bladder complaints, Moira thought to herself. 'Thanks a million, Alasdair.'

He pulled a chair out for her and waited while she slipped out of her coat and handed it to him before sitting down.

'Needing a dose of your Tom counts as an emergency,' Alasdair said flapping a napkin out and placing it across her lap. 'Right, my Greek goddess, I'm sure your fella or Paula will be over to take your order in a moment or two. Enjoy.' He blew her a kiss and migrated back to his post by the door. She watched, amused, as his arms opened wide to greet two dolly birds who'd appeared in the entrance.

Where'd she get the phrase dolly birds? she wondered, frowning as she picked up the carafe of water. It was the sort of thing Mammy would say. God, she was only three months gone and she was already saying mammyish things.

She settled herself in for a spot of people watching but her eyes settled on Tom who was weaving around the laden tables over to where a lardy lad in a suit was waving at him. Moira pitied him his task. By the looks of the fella, he'd have come straight from work drinks and was probably three sheets to the wind. She remembered those days only too well.

You had to have patience and a mild manner to serve the public, Moira thought watching the scene unfold. She didn't have either. If your red-nosed man over there started giving out to her she'd tell him to feck off with himself or he'd find a sausage where the sun don't shine.

This was why she wasn't a waitress. She had broached it once with Aisling, asking her to put a good word in Quinn's ear as she could do with supplementing her limited student allowance. Aisling had snorted which Moira had taken as a 'not on your life'.

Tom's ability to smile and keep calm would serve him well in his chosen profession once he qualified, she mused. He'd make an excellent doctor. And, she thought, glancing down at her non-existent midriff, a good daddy. At the very thought, her tummy did a somersault.

She wondered how long she'd get away with the little black dress she was currently wearing. Would she get cankles and have to wear sensible shoes? What would she look like with a big belly?

Probably like a younger version of Bronagh and Mammy she decided.

Her gaze sharpened and her shoulders tensed as she saw a woman nudge her pal. They were like hunters in a safari park as they logged Tom's movements, or rather his undulating buttocks. She'd have been jealous except he never gave her any reason to be.

Tom, bless him, was completely oblivious to the effect he and his bum had on the opposite and, she thought, glancing towards the door at Alasdair, same sex.

She wondered, while she waited for him to turn around so she could wave out, whether she'd ever stop noticing his backside. Would they grow grumpy and complacent with one another? She'd heard it said that when you had a great view to look at every single day you stopped noticing it after a while. It was just there.

She couldn't imagine a day coming where she'd not want to grope Tom's bum. She made a promise to herself, no matter how up to her eyeballs in baby sick and nappies she got, she'd always find time to cop a feel.

She and his admirers observed Tom demonstrate his best customer service skills as he placated the arse in the suit and once he had him smiling and nodding, obviously happy with Tom's suggestions, he turned away. Moira knew him well enough to spot the set of his jaw but it softened when he saw her wave and his face creased into a broad grin.

He looked like he'd be more at home on a surfboard in Australia than in a quaint Irish bistro. His honey coloured hair was pulled back into a loose ponytail and he'd the sort of skin that looked as though he'd been on his hols in the depth of winter.

He made a beeline in her direction and she stood up to greet him, her nerve endings jangling with the anticipation of what was to come.

He pulled her close and gave her a long kiss. 'You smell gorgeous.'

She should do, she thought, she'd had a very generous squirt of Aisling's perfume. 'You smell like onions.' She grinned up at him despite standing taller than usual because she'd also commandeered Aisling's red Gucci sandals. She couldn't help herself, they went so well with her dress. This was another reason she'd legged it from the apartment earlier.

He grinned. 'And sausages too probably, there's been a run on bangers 'n' mash tonight.'

'It's a good job, I like onions and sausages then, isn't it?'

His soft, hazel eyes gave her the once over. 'You look beautiful, Moira. That dress does things to me.'

Moira preened, pleased he'd noticed.

'What are you doing here though? I thought we were meeting at mine once my shift ended.'

'We were but I didn't feel like an evening in with Aisling banging on about ovaries and the like.' The irony of what she'd just said didn't escape her. She knew, though, if she'd said, *we need to talk*, he'd have thought she was planning on breaking up with him.

It occurred to her then that Aisling was desperate to be in the position Moira had unwittingly found herself in. She wondered how she'd take the news her younger sister had gotten there first.

'Fair play to you.' Tom's eyes flicked over at the kitchen. 'Between you and me I think she's driving Quinn demented with all her temperature taking and—

'Sexual demands. She's insatiable,' Moira added with a matter-of-fact nod of her head. 'Ash gets a bee in her bonnet and she fixates on it. Sure, look at the way she can never let things go. She still harps on about a scratch I supposedly got on her Valentino slingbacks and that was over a year ago. If she just relaxed and thought of England instead of babies, she'd be grand.'

Tom laughed. 'I wasn't going to word it quite like that but that's the gist of it right enough. Quinn's exhausted. He told me if he has to eat another oyster he'll be sick so he will.'

Moira grimaced. She wasn't a fan of the crustacean and even if she was, she was sure she'd heard it said shellfish, when you were pregnant, wasn't a good idea. Come to think of it there were probably a few things she was supposed to avoid now. She'd have to make an appointment with her doctor. Mind you, Mammy was sure to be a mine of information. She sighed, remembering her helpful tips when Roisin had been expecting Noah. She'd driven her sister demented and she'd been in London at the time!

'You picked a good night to come down.' Tom interrupted her thoughts. 'The band's supposed to be great. Do you want a glass of lemonade or a coke?'

That was one thing, Moira thought, she'd not have to give up the drink. She'd done that a while ago now and was all the better for it.

'A lemonade would be grand, thanks.'

'Have you eaten?'

'No.'

'Family discount. Choose something.'

Quinn was generous like that, Moira thought. She'd have normally felt guilty about taking advantage of his good nature by ordering the beef and Guinness stew with extra dumplings (she was eating for two) but figured she deserved it having put up with his and Ash's headboard banging these last months.

Tom disappeared to take her order through to the kitchen before returning with the lemonade she'd requested. He couldn't hang about as another table had just been seated and so, with a lingering kiss, he left her to wait for her meal.

Moira whiled away the time waiting for her dinner imagining her and Tom with a flat of their own and a plump little baby who smiled it's gappy baby smile up at them and never cried. She'd not be one of those mammies forever after complaining how hard it all was, she vowed, as Paula placed her aromatic stew down in front of her.

'Quinn says hello and enjoy. The kitchen's a madhouse or he'd have come out with this himself.'

Moira shrugged it was fine and thanked Paula before tucking in. She was starved!

The next time Tom breezed over to her table she'd all but licked her plate clean.

He took it with a raised eyebrow. 'Jaysus, Moira, I don't know where you put it.'

Moira squirmed. She was feeling too full and she could feel the ominous rumblings of indigestion. She'd have to have a glass of the bicarb when she got back to Tom's. Mammy swore by it for the heartburn.

Tom carried her plate towards the kitchen, stopping to clear another table as the band struck up. They were good, Moira thought, her toes tapping as she watched the small area reserved for dancing fill up. She liked a dance but tonight she wasn't in the mood.

By the time the Fiddling Feehans were in the midst of their last set, she'd had enough. She was beginning to wish she'd gone straight round to Tom's to wait for him there. She could have been sitting up in bed, tele on with a cup of tea, working her way through the packet of Jaffa cakes Tamar always had in the cupboard. It was a much more enticing prospect than listening to yer mad fiddlers up there, she thought, yawning.

There was no point leaving now though. She'd have to pay for a taxi for one thing; a stupid expense given Tom's car was parked out the back. She'd have to wait it out.

She clapped especially loudly when the band finally took a bow and exited the stage.

The revellers trickled out the door slowly in search of late-night entertainment and once Alasdair had locked the door behind the last of them, Moira got up. She was happy to help clear a few tables now there was no one around.

'Thanks, Moira,' Paula called, stacking the glasswasher behind the bar area.

Moira, balancing plates and dessert bowls, tottered through to the kitchen. Quinn looked up from where he was making sure his new kitchen hand did a good job of wiping the worktops down. 'Alright there, Moira. Do you fancy talking Tom into staying for a staff drink?'

'No, I don't. I'm knackered so I am. It's home for us. It was a grand stew, by the way, it really hit the spot.' It was hitting the wrong spot now though, she thought, swallowing down the reflux. She never usually got indigestion. 'And anyway, Quinn Moran, you should be getting off home yourself. Aisling will be waiting up for you. You've a job to be doing.'

A flicker Moira couldn't pinpoint crossed her brother-in-law's face and she made a note to self to tell Aisling to ease off on the whole baby-making thing because she was driving her husband mad.

'I suppose you're right.'

'That's the last of it, Quinn. We'll be off then,' Tom said, shrugging into his jacket and fishing his keys from his pocket. 'Ready, Moira?'

She fetched her coat from where Alasdair had hung it in the cloakroom and nodded. They said their goodnights to everyone and ventured out into the night air, cool after all the heat the dancing bodies had generated.

The Fiddling Feehans were packing up their van, Moira saw, as Tom draped an arm around her shoulder. She liked the way she fitted in under it just so. They were a good fit her and Tom. He was whistling one of the tunes the band had been playing as he led her across the car park.

He'd no clue what was coming, Moira thought, with a pang of apprehension. It had been a shock for her alright but she'd had two months of suspecting something was afoot. Sliding into the passenger seat of his battered old Ford, she told herself she was being silly.

Sure, he'd be delighted once he'd had a chance to get used to the idea. He had to be because she'd no clue what she'd do if he wasn't.

Chapter Ten

The two-storey, brick house Tom shared with Malcolm and Tamar in Ranelagh sat in a row of identical two-storey, brick houses down a quiet side street. The only point of difference was the front gardens behind the wrought iron gates. Some were well-tended, some were not. Tom and his flatmates' was not.

The first time Moira had stayed at Tom's she'd been reminded of an unfortunate incident a few years earlier when she'd been in her party girl prime. On this particular Saturday night, she'd necked more than a skinful and had barged into her then boyfriend's house calling out, 'I'm hot to trot, gee-up, Neddy,' only to find an elderly couple in the front room watching the Late Late Show on the tele. She'd been too tanked to be mortified, that had set in later. She'd broken up with Ned not long after. It was no bad thing. She could never have stuck with anyone called Ned for the long haul.

Waiting for Tom to turn the key in the lock, she shivered. She did not miss those days of waking up with a banging head as the fragments of her misdemeanours the night before slowly pieced themselves together.

The house was in darkness and Tom put his fingers to his lips. Moira jumped but managed to hold back a squeal as Tamar's witchy black cat Kismet brushed past her legs and began to mewl.

The cat's yellow eyes glowed in the dark as she waited haughtily to be petted. Moira didn't oblige. She loved animals, she really did, but Kismet had this knack of making her feel as though she were getting a feline hex put on her each time she looked her way. She'd not moved on from the sweater threading incident either and wasn't appeased by Tamar insisting she take it as a compliment because Kismet only clawed people she liked.

Tom whispered at the cat to quieten down and she stomped off in the direction of the kitchen, clearly hoping someone would give her a midnight snack. They took to the stairs instead.

Tamar and Malcolm were such swots, Moira thought, as they stepped onto the landing. There was no sliver of light shining under their doors. It was only a few minutes after midnight on the weekend and they both had their lights out, sound asleep no doubt.

Tom flicked on his bedroom light and closing the door behind him pulled her into his arms. 'I've been trying to keep my hands off you all night.' He breathed into her hair. 'Now what's under that coat.' He undid the belt and helped her out of it.

Moira would have giggled but her indigestion had her feeling out of sorts.

'I think I might need some bicarb. I've got awful heartburn.'

Nothing like telling a man you'd indigestion to quell his ardour she thought as Tom slung her coat down on the bed and backed off. 'Poor you. Mind you did shovel that stew down. I don't know about bicarb but I think there's some Mylanta in the medicine kit. Back in a tick.' He tossed his jacket onto the chair by the window with practised ease and Moira sat down on the bed to wait while he ventured back down the stairs.

She could feel her breath getting shallower and faster as her anxiety began to heighten while she waited. Do the bendy yoga, belly breathing like Rosi's shown you, she told herself listening out for the telltale creak on the stairs to tell her he was on his way back up.

How should she play this? Should she try and pretend she didn't feel as though her innards were sitting in her throat and feign amorousness. Would the news there would be three in their relationship in just over five months be better received post ride? Hmm, maybe not, she thought, her nails digging into her palms. Tom was notorious for falling asleep straight after. Once he'd even done so on top of her. She hadn't realised until he'd started snoring.

There was no time to dwell on it further because he reappeared holding a capful of Mylanta out to her. 'Thanks.' She downed it in one gulp.

Tom began to undress and she eyed him as he took his shirt off and undid his jeans. He'd them down around his knees when her mouth took on a life of its own as the words, 'I'm pregnant,' spilled forth into the quiet bedroom.

He froze with his jeans still hovering at half-mast as if in a quandary as to whether to pull them up or down. There was absolute silence until a scratching and mewling began to sound outside the door. Moira breathed, 'Feck off with you, Kismet.'

Tom cracked an oafish grin. 'Good one, Moira, you had me then.'

Moira sighed. 'Why would I joke about something like that? I'm nearly three months, I think. Do you remember the night before I left for LA?'

She could see the cogs turning as he decided keeping his trousers on was a safer bet.

It was too late for that now though, she thought, watching him zip them back up.

The expression of horror on his face made her defensive and she had to bite back the words, 'don't you remember I told you no glove no love'. He'd wheedled his way around her though, assuring her he'd pull out in time. He'd better up his game with his contraceptive advice when he qualified, she thought, or Ireland would be in for another baby boom. She waited for him to say something.

'I told you you'd be better off taking the pill.'

'Tom,' she spluttered, irritation flaring as he held his index finger to his lips to shush her. There was nothing worse than being shushed when your blood was boiling and she fought to control her volume. 'I told you what happened the last time I went on that. I wound up growing hair where hair should not be growing. I wouldn't have needed to stay on the fecking pill because you'd not want to do the riding with a bearded woman anyway.'

She watched Tom's shoulders slump. This was not going how she'd wanted it to go. Why had he not pulled her into his arms and said, 'What a surprise! And sure, it's not planned, Moira, but the best things in life never are. We'll be grand. I love you, babe.'

Instead, he was glaring at her as if it were all her fault. Tom was being an arse. 'You're being an arse,' she said.

'I don't know what you want me to say, Moira. I mean you land this on me out the blue on a Friday night after I've just come off a long shift. I'm hardly going to be jumping for joy now, am I? We're in no position to be having a baby. Jaysus, I didn't see that on the cards for at least another ten years.'

'Life doesn't run to a timetable,' she protested. 'Things happen and people step up and get on with it.'

'But I'm not ready to be a dad.'

'And I'm not ready to be a mam but we've got five months to get ourselves ready.'

Tom began shaking his head slowly. 'I don't want a baby, not yet, Moira.'

'What are you saying?' Her blood had turned icy.

'You just said you're not three months yet. There's still time for a termination. I'll come with you to England. It will be over before you know it.' There was a desperate glint in his eyes. 'You're right, it happens. People make mistakes but it doesn't have to change anything between us.'

Moira couldn't believe what she was hearing. 'But don't you see, Tom, it changes everything.' She felt betrayed by the hot, salty tears sliding down her face.

'Ah, Moira, come on now, think with your head. We're not ready for this.'

'No, Tom. It's you who's not ready for this.' Moira swiped her coat up from the bed and thrust her arms back into it not bothering to belt it in her hurry to grab her bag. She needed to put distance between them and she resisted the urge to bang his door closed behind her as she took to the stairs.

Half of her wanted him to come running down after her, full of apologies about how it had been the shock of it all that had him behaving like so but the door didn't open behind her. She cursed as she nearly tripped over Kismet before reaching the front door and, stepping out into the quiet, dark street she dug her phone out of her bag. She'd ring a taxi and go. Go where? She wanted her mammy, Moira realised.

Chapter Eleven

'Donal, there's someone knocking on the door,' Maureen slurred, her voice thick with sleep. She'd been in the middle of a lovely dream whereby she and Donal were being gracious hosts in their resplendent new seaside manor house.

She'd basically replayed a scene from the romance novel bookmarked on the bedside table. The only difference was Donal wasn't a Cornish lord with a roguish past. He was a retired gasfitter who sang in a Kenny Rogers tribute band and she loved him just the way he was. Mind you the roguish part had been getting exciting. She forced herself to focus on what had woken her up and shook Donal who had a silly smile on his face. A happy snore erupted from him but he still didn't wake. She wondered what he was dreaming about.

The knocking sounded again. It was a sharp retort in the silence of the apartment. The noise had roused Pooh who'd begun yapping indignantly at the interruption.

Donal stirred at the barking and a spear of fear pierced Maureen's foggy mind. It wasn't the norm for people to be knocking on people's doors in the middle of the night unless it was an emergency of some sort. She hauled herself upright and flicked on the bedside lamp blinking at the sudden brightness.

'Donal, wake up,' she whispered urgently, unsure why she was whispering. 'There's someone at the door and it's after midnight.' She shook him again until he spluttered awake properly and swinging his legs off the bed, he sat up, rubbing his eyes before staggering forth on automatic pilot.

Maureen stumbled after him clutching his dressing gown. If it were the gards on the other side of the door they didn't need to be greeted by Donal in his underpants. He'd obviously been having a very happy dream she thought helping him into the robe and belting it before his hand reached for the door.

Maureen hung back, her face pinched and pale as she peered around him to see who was standing there.

'How're you, Donal. Sorry it's so late. Is my mammy about?'

'Moira, what are you doing here?' Maureen nudged Donal aside to see her youngest child standing there looking like she was about to flash them both in her trench coat. Maureen's eagle eye took note of the tear tracks through her daughter's makeup.

'Can I stay here with you and Donal, Mammy? I had words with Tom. He's such an arse.'

Maureen reached out and pulled her inside. 'Come on in with you, we don't want the neighbours hearing our business.' They'd think she and Donal were up to the kinky business if they caught sight of Moira in the flasher coat.

Before she had a chance to lock the door behind her though, Moira asked for money.

'It's for the taxi fare, Mammy. The driver's waiting out the front of the building. I promised him I'd be back down in a sec.' A very nice driver man he'd been too, listening to her pouring her heart out about commitment-phobic arsy boyfriends all the way from Ranelagh to Howth.

'How much is it?'

Moira muttered a sum that had Maureen clutching her heart. 'Jaysus wept, Moira. It's daylight robbery so it is.'

'It's night time actually, Mammy.'

Maureen's eyes slitted as she stared her daughter down. Given the hour, and the sum of money she'd just requested, she was in no position to be making the clever remarks. 'Donal have you any large notes on you, I don't have enough to cover her fare.' She turned in the hope Donal could help them out so as the neighbours weren't treated to the sight of a flasher and an irate taxi driver.

Donal had already padded into the living area to fetch his wallet from his jacket pocket and was pulling out a wodge of cash which he pressed into Moira's hand. 'That should cover it, Moira.'

'Thanks a million, Donal. I'll pay you back.' Moira took off for the lift and Maureen watched her go. 'She won't, you know. I suppose we should put the kettle on and find out what's been going on.'

Donal had read her mind once more and was already making for the kitchen to do just that. She was a lucky woman, Maureen thought, sitting down heavily on the sofa to await the return of her prodigal daughter.

A puffing Moira burst through the door a few minutes later. 'All sorted, thank you.'

'Would you like a sugar in your tea, Moira?'

'I don't know about her, Donal, but I would. Sugar's good for the shock like,' Maureen said.

'What shock?' Moira sat down next to her mammy.

'What shock?' Maureen snorted. 'The shock of you being in the family way for one thing, not to mention showing up here in the middle of the night. I thought it was the gardai come with terrible news.'

'I've put two sugars in, Maureen,' Donal said, placing her cup down on the occasional table next to her. 'And one for you, Moira.'

Moira smiled her gratitude.

'I'll head off back to bed so you two can have a chat,' Donal said, resting his hand briefly on Maureen's shoulder. She reached up and patted it.

She waited until their bedroom door clicked shut before turning her attention to Moira who was looking exhausted in her opinion. 'Now, what's been going on with you and Tom?'

Moira opened her mouth, fully intending to tell her mammy what had happened but instead of words, a noisy sob escaped. She began to weep as the enormity of the day piled in on top of her.

'Ah, Moira, come here.' Maureen pulled her daughter to her and Moira snuggled in, comforted by the familiar faint scent of Arpège. Bit by bit she relayed their conversation.

'The lad got a shock, Moira. Sure, I got a shock but I'm coming around and he will too. I'm sure once he's had time to think things through he'll be on the phone trying to patch things up with you. Tom loves you so he does. I've seen the way he looks at you.' It was true Maureen thought, he was smitten. It was the way he hung off Moira's every word as though she'd said something profound like Mother Theresa or your Gandhi one when in fact she was usually talking absolute rubbish. Moira had had an inkling something was amiss when she missed her monthlies but for Tom, it would have come out of the blue.

'He loves me, Mammy, just not enough,' Moira said tearfully.

'There, there.' Maureen patted her back just like she had when she was a baby with the windy-pops. 'Come on now. We'll not solve anything sitting up half the night. Drink your tea and then I'll tuck you in. How does that sound?'

'Would I be allowed a chocolate biscuit too, Mammy?' Moira asked, wiping her wet cheeks. 'For the shock like.'

'Go on then. You know where the tin is.'

Moira got up and made a beeline for the kitchen. She helped herself to four biscuits just in case Mammy made her hand one over and then sat down to finish her tea.

'Moira, that's greedy so it is. Give me one.'

They sat in silence finishing their tea and the biscuits and Moira was surprised to find the chocolate and the sugar did have a soothing effect. By the time Mammy ordered her off to bed she was feeling calmer and ready to try and get some sleep.

'I'll fetch you one of my nighties,' Maureen said after she'd turned the covers down on the guest bed for Moira. She tiptoed off in the direction of her bedroom.

She returned with a chin-to-toe nightie muttering something about if she wore gowns like this to bed instead of those wispy bits of material that wound up lodged in places where fabric had no right to be, she wouldn't have been up to the out of wedlock shenanigans in the first place.

Moira didn't bite back; she was too tired and, kicking Aisling's shoes under the bed, she slipped out of her dress vowing never to wear the fecking thing ever again before pulling the chaste nightgown over her head. She couldn't be bothered taking her makeup off or rubbing toothpaste across her teeth. She wanted to sleep and forget tonight had happened.

She clambered into bed and held her arms up so as Maureen could tuck her in the way she used to when she was small. 'Pull them tight, Mammy,' she ordered.

Maureen dutifully tugged the sheets so there wasn't a wrinkle in them and tucked her daughter in. She sat down on the side of the bed, red in the face from the effort.

'Do you want me to sit with you for a while, Moira? I could sing you the train whistle blowing song.'

'Mammy, I'm twenty-six.'

'I know that, Moira, but you're never too old for the train whistle blowing song. It was your favourite.'

'Alright, Mammy, sing the song,' Moira said, struggling to keep her eyes open.

It was all the invitation Maureen needed and she launched into her country and western version of Train Whistle Blowing.

Moira cringed at the yee-haw she added after the bit about the captain being at the engine but despite her mammy's ad-libbing she began to drift off. She was warm, she was safe, and she was loved. She'd be alright.

Maureen's gaze was soft as she soaked in the sight of her daughter. She looked so young and vulnerable she thought, watching her breathe in that measured way that signalled she was asleep. She shook her head and, reaching down, stroked her warm cheek gently. How could it be that her baby was having a baby?

Chapter Twelve

Aisling was lying in bed staring at the ceiling. Her eyes were burning with tiredness but her brain was refusing to give in and let her sleep. She kept replaying the events of the day.

Things had gotten off to a bad start thanks to Mr Timbs and his wife. They'd travelled from Tipperary for a weekend city break in Dublin.

Aisling had the couple pegged within minutes of them checking in. It was in the dissatisfied aura coming off the pair in waves. She'd said she'd put money on them finding something unsatisfactory about their room within the hour to Bronagh once they were out of earshot. She'd their number alright. They were the sort of joyless couple who'd pick holes where there were none to be picked.

She'd been proved right when Mrs Timbs had rung down to reception ten minutes later to complain there was a dust-ball under their bed. Aisling who personally checked the rooms after Ita had made them up knew if there was it would be the size of an ant. Nevertheless, the customer was always right and so she'd apologised and sent a po-faced Ita in to hoover the room once more while she made the Timbs a cup of tea in the guests' lounge.

She'd winced hearing Ita smacking into the skirtings overhead with the vacuum cleaner at the slur on her cleaning habits. Aisling knew though, if she didn't keep a beady eye on their director of housekeeping, standards at the guesthouse would slip.

Then, this morning, Mr Timbs had cornered her as his wife headed downstairs for breakfast to sniff that the so-called power shower could only be described as a tepid trickle at best.

Aisling prided herself on her professionalism and as such, she'd not replied, 'Feck off with you, any hotter and the water would scald the skin off you.' Oh no, that was Moira's style, not hers which was why she'd mustered up her sweetest smile and assured him she'd look into it.

Appeased, but eager for something else to complain about, he'd trotted down the stairs to the dining room for a full Irish.

Aisling had appeared in time to see Mrs Timbs, sausage wobbling on her fork, calling Mrs Flaherty over. She'd surmised she was intending to tell the cook the pork banger wasn't to her liking. Upon seeing the robust Mrs Flaherty bearing down on her as she rolled up her sleeves like she was about to embark on a bare-knuckle fistfight the woman had put her fork down and choked out, 'My compliments to the cook,' instead.

Things had gone from bad to worse in Aisling's day when she'd headed off to meet Dave, the Viking tour operator, by the banks of the Liffey early in the afternoon.

'I only answer to Erik the Viking when I'm working,' he'd whispered, helping her board a boat she wasn't sure was sea or river worthy.

She should have known he was running a shonky operation by the horned hat to which he'd superglued a red beard and she was fairly sure the enormous codpiece she'd been prodded with as she boarded was more Middle Ages than Viking.

Reliving the moment the boat had tipped ominously, thanks to her with the enormous thighs jumping aboard as though she were competing in the hurdles, she shuddered in the darkened bedroom. She'd come a hair's breadth from winding up in the murky water next to the shopping trolleys and whatever else lurked in its depths.

Moira had been acting peculiar this evening too, now that she thought about it. She'd been snappy and she'd skulked around before heading out the door like she'd a firecracker up her arse. Perhaps it was that time of the month. Aisling mustered up a frisson of sympathy. She wasn't sweetness and light when she was due on either. Especially not lately.

Her ears strained but the apartment was silent apart from her own huffy breathing which was getting huffier by the minute. Quinn should have been home ages ago. She'd waited up for him, expecting to hear his key in the lock any moment but the minutes had turned into an hour then an hour had passed and now annoyance at his lack of consideration was settling in.

He could have called and told her he was planning on staying after hours for a few work drinks, he'd have known she'd be waiting up for him. Surely she wasn't that much of a shrew that he felt he couldn't.

A rattling followed by a clatter sounded and a smile tugged at her mouth despite her irritation. She knew what it was and tossing the covers aside she felt her way over to the window. Pulling back the curtain, the window groaned in protest as she pushed it up so as she could peer down into the courtyard below.

The sensor light had been tripped because, just as she'd expected, Mr Fox had decided to pay their bin a visit. Spotlighted he stared up at her, caught in the middle of his bacon rind heist. She knew she should hiss at him to go away if she didn't want to be subjected to Mrs Flaherty's rolling pin ranting about the mess he'd left behind in the morning. Then she remembered it was Friday and the milder mannered Mrs Baicu would be working in the kitchen tomorrow.

'It's your lucky night, Mr Fox. Go for your life,' she whispered.

Mr Fox gave her a flick of his bushy red tail before nose-diving into his nirvana once more. She waited and watched as he bobbed back up like a foxy version of Oscar the Grouch and, satisfied with his haul, slinked over to his hole under the wall.

Aisling closed the window and mooched back to bed, throwing herself down and wrenching the covers over her. What did it matter if Quinn came home now anyway? She certainly wasn't in the mood for the riding. She was in the mood for stewing and thinking unkind thoughts about him.

She found herself doing something she hadn't done in a long while:

Dear Aisling,

My husband and I are trying for a baby. I've been very enthusiastic about this as at 37 years of age, I don't feel time is on my side. I know in the grand scale of things we haven't been trying long and that for some couples it can take years but it's all I think about. It's not healthy and it's not helping. The thing is I haven't been married a year and my husband is beginning to stop out late to avoid me. I think all my pushing is seeing him pull away but I don't know how else to be because if I don't keep at him how will I get pregnant? What should I do?

Yours faithfully,

Me

Her inner voice of reason told her it would happen and she was being ridiculous but it didn't help and she squeezed her eyes shut opening them a crack when the click of the door opening signalled Quinn was home, finally.

Instead of flicking the light on and launching at him for being a selfish stop-out as she'd been lying there planning, she found herself closing her eyes and feigning sleep. She was suddenly frightened to ask him what he thought he was playing at for fear she wouldn't like what he had to say.

Chapter Thirteen

Maureen put the hairdryer back on its hook and liberally sprayed her can of strong-hold hairspray, her eyes watering in protest at the mist descending. She angled the magnifying mirror she favoured these days for the best light in order to put on her makeup.

It was disconcerting to see one's imperfections magnified like so. She'd much preferred applying her makeup in ignorant fuzzy bliss but she'd given in and bought the mirror after the girls had told her she'd a whisker on her chin that was five centimetres long.

Aisling had been particularly annoying, reciting The Three Little Pigs word for word. She'd told her she'd swing for her if she sang the not by the hair of my chinny chin chin song one more time.

Frowning at the memory, she swept on her mascara and lipstick, double-checked her chin, and then satisfied she was presentable, exited the bathroom.

She paused outside the guest room hearing Moira's snores. She wished she'd a recorder to hand because Moira refused to believe she'd a freight train snore on her when she got going. How her poor Tom got any sleep was beyond her. That was when she remembered Moira and Tom had had words last night which was why her daughter was presently raising the ceiling in her spare bedroom.

Things always looked brighter in the light of day she reassured herself. Sure, the pair of them would sit down and talk things through like adults. They were going to have to because it wasn't just about them. It was about her grandchild too and if they didn't sort it out she'd step in and play the role of Judge Judy. Only, her form of mediation would involve the banging of heads together to see sense.

She hesitated, her hand on the doorknob. Should she wake Moira and tell her to get round to Tom's now to sort things out? Strike while the iron was hot. No, Moira was a short-tempered madam when she'd not had enough sleep. Best leave her, she decided, her hand dropping to her side as she recalled the dark circles under her daughter's eyes. She'd looked like an Irish cousin of that Roger Racoon fella they'd met in LA. A few extra hours kip wouldn't do her any harm.

Aware of Donal moving about in the kitchen, Maureen followed her nose in that direction. He liked to cook breakfast of a Saturday and Sunday morning. They were settling into their routines nicely, she thought fondly. She did the cereal and toast of a week and he did the eggs and bacon of a weekend. She hoovered, he dusted, she played the tambourine, he sang. There was a song in there somewhere she thought, smiling as Donal looked up.

He'd the spatula in his hand. 'Scrambled eggs do you, Maureen? The bacon's crispy, just how you like it. And I made a pot of the plunger coffee.'

She inhaled the rich French roast blend he liked. 'Lovely, you spoil me, Donal.'

He grinned. 'There's no one else I'd rather spoil. Will Moira be joining us?'

'No, she's sound asleep. I'll let her have a lie in. She can sort herself out when she gets up.'

Donal nodded and began scraping the eggs onto the toast before retrieving the bacon he'd had warming in the oven.

Pooh minced over deciding to try his luck. He plonked himself at Donal's feet with a baleful expression on his face. Donal knew it'd take more than a crunchy bit of rind to win the dog over but God loved a trier. He slipped him a piece knowing full well the next time he looked at the dog he'd have his sharp little, poodly teeth bared in his direction ready for the nipping when Maureen wasn't looking.

Maureen caught sight of herself reflected in the window, mentally adding another line to her song which had taken on the tune of yer tomato tomata one. She cleaned the windows, he washed the dishes.

She'd dressed in what had become her house viewing uniform. Mo-pants teamed with a mauve cashmere sweater and a jauntily tied pink silk scarf knotted around her neck in a final flourish to complete the look. The method behind her madness was silk and cashmere were luxury materials therefore they gave off a 'we're cashed up seniors who are serious' vibe. As for the Mo-pants, well she wasn't one to miss a marketing opportunity.

Sure, the best way to sell them was to wear them.

Only last week she'd had to get Rosi to send a stack of them over because she'd sold out and had a waiting list getting longer by the day.

The agent that had shown them around the house (shack) on the hill with magnificent sea views (if you used a NASA quality telescope) had put her name down for a pair after

Maureen demonstrated her lunges in what had constituted a kitchen.

'I have to say, Mo, you look fresh as a daisy given our night. Is she alright?' Donal inclined his head towards the hall where the bedrooms were located on either side.

'She'll be grand. A lovers tiff, that's all. She took Tom by surprise with her news. You're looking very suave today too, Donal.' Maureen was grateful as she blew Donal a cheeky kiss that Moira was still in bed; she'd have been making the gagging noises if she were here to witness their exchange.

Donal carried their plates over to the table while Maureen set about pouring the strong, aromatic brew. 'We don't have to go, Mo. If you'd rather stay here until Moira gets up we can always reschedule our appointment.'

'No, Moira's a big girl. Sure, she's going to be a mammy, isn't she? She'll have to learn to look after herself if she's to look after a little one. Besides, I've a feeling this house could be the one.'

Donal, bless him, didn't add that she'd said this about the twelve other houses they'd gone to look at. She tucked into her breakfast with gusto.

Despite her words, as Donal tidied the breakfast dishes away, Maureen telephoned Aisling.

'Aisling, it's your mammy.'

Aisling resisted the bad word that threatened. She should have been downstairs half an hour ago but had overslept. Quinn had left at the crack of dawn for a game of golf with his brother despite his late night. He'd bounded out of bed like a gazelle. She'd had to drag herself out having banged off the alarm and gone back to sleep. It had taken her forever to go off last night. She'd laid next to her husband, seething, as he happily gave off boozy-breathed, snuffly snores.

'Aisling, are you there?' Maureen demanded.

'Yes, Mammy.' She rubbed her temples. She could've been the one with the hangover and she wasn't in the mood for Mammy. 'I thought you were going to see about a house with Donal this morning?'

'We'll be heading off in a minute but I wondered if you'd ring here in an hour?'

'Why? What's the point if you're not going to be there?' Aisling was suspicious because, knowing Mammy, she'd probably trained Pooh to answer the fecking thing. She'd be after getting her to chat to him so as he didn't get lonely while she and Donal were out. 'Can you not just put the country music on for him like you normally do?'

'What are you talking about?'

'Pooh of course. What are you on about?'

'Aisling, pay attention. I never mentioned Pooh. I'm after wanting you to call Moira. She had words with Tom last night and camped out in our spare room.'

'Ah, she'll be grand, Mammy. You know what Moira's like, a drama queen.' Aisling flapped her hand dismissively. She'd bigger things on her mind than Moira squabbling with Tom over something trivial.

'True enough but she was awfully upset and there's more to it than just a tiff.'

Aisling toyed with the phone cord. There was a caginess to Mammy's tone. 'What's going on?'

Maureen spied Donal picking up his car keys. 'I don't have time to get into it with you. We'll talk about it at the family conference this afternoon. But in the meantime, will you just do what I asked of you?'

'What family conference?'

'The family conference scheduled at O'Mara's for four o'clock this afternoon. I've done the maths, Patrick can join us on the phone, it'll be eight in the morning in Los Angeles and Rosi should be about then too.'

'Jaysus, Mammy, what are you on about, family conference? What's going on? You can't leave me hanging like that all day thinking the worst.' Aisling was alarmed now.

'It's nothing for you to fret over. It's not life or death.' Actually, Maureen thought, technically it was the former. She elaborated. 'Nobody's sick or anything like that. Now would you just tell me you'll ring your sister?' Maureen mouthed at Donal 'Give me one second.'

'Alright, alright, I'll call her. But listen, Mammy, will we be having drinks and nibbles and the like too.'

'No, Aisling, a family conference is a serious business, not a social event.'

Ah-ha, gotcha, Aisling thought. 'But you just said it was nothing for me to fret about.'

Maureen clenched her jaw, speaking through gritted teeth. 'Stop debating with me. I've got to go. Just do as you've been told and ring your sister.' She put the phone down with a clunk.

Aisling stared at the receiver. She'd give it five and she'd ring Moira. She'd get to the bottom of what was going on. There was no way she was waiting until four o'clock.

Chapter Fourteen

The property they were winding their way up the hill behind Howth to view was called Mornington Mews. Maureen didn't know what a mews was exactly but she did know it sounded posh. Therefore, she was excited and had pushed Moira to the back of her mind, for the morning at least.

The advertisement had proclaimed this mysterious mews property to have majestic harbour views along with a private south-facing garden. There were the requisite three bedrooms they were after and Donal, having lived with a wife and two daughters, was adamant two bathrooms was non-negotiable.

It was Donal who'd spotted the ad as he'd flicked through the paper. He'd called Maureen over and they'd ticked all their wish list boxes before telephoning to make an appointment with Agent Colleen to view it.

As soon as Maureen had read the property was listed with an Agent Colleen she'd wanted to add FBI Special Agent to Colleen's title. She'd been watching too many American crime dramas of late and that was down to Donal. Still and all, a successful relationship was about compromise. It couldn't all be *Fair City* and *Bally K* now they were cohabitating.

The black and white photograph in the paper had showed a grand olde-worlde sprawling home which had been carved into smaller residences. They'd agreed the developers had done a good job of retaining the country charm even though it wasn't actually in the country. It could be the perfect compromise between Maureen's apartment and Donal's suburban family home.

One thing they'd learned since they'd begun their hunt for the perfect place though was estate agents were wordsmiths and if a photograph was taken from a good angle when the sun was out the tumbledown garden shed could look like somewhere you'd want to go and see your bank manager about.

So, with all this in mind, Maureen was trying not to get her hopes up. Mornington Mews did have a lovely ring to it, she thought, gazing at the fat white clouds scudding overhead. She put on her telephone voice in her head and said, 'Maureen O'Mara of Mornington Mews here.' *Oh yes a lovely ring.*

It was a beautiful day, she thought. Far too beautiful for Moira and Tom to be at odds; they'd make things up, she reassured herself, and then remembered she wasn't going to think about them until after she and Donal saw the house.

'Number sixty-five, here we are.' Donal indicated and crunched onto an expanse of gravel drive. Leafy foliage blocked their initial view of the house but, as they rounded a bend, there it was.

Maureen gasped and grabbed Donal's arm which saw him skid on the gravel as he slammed his foot down on the brakes. Their heads bobbed back and forth with the sudden motion. It wasn't the grand arrival she'd had in mind.

'Sorry about that, Maureen.'

Now wasn't the time to be terse though, and to maintain a successful relationship you had to be prepared to admit when you were wrong. 'Not at all, Donal, I shouldn't have grabbed you like so when you're behind the wheel.'

They re-gathered their equilibrium and Donal inched the car sedately in behind a highly polished red number they were guessing belonged to Agent Colleen who was meeting them here.

Mews, in this case, Maureen saw, clambering out the car eager to inspect it, meant a converted Edwardian manor house. It had been divided into three smart townhouses. The house they'd come to view was the end closest to where the hill they were on sloped away and the crisply painted door had just been flung wide.

'Mornington Mews welcomes you!' A woman squeezed into a trouser suit beamed a horsey smile at them as she gestured for them to come hither. 'You must be Donal and Maureen. I'm Agent Colleen.'

FBI Special Agent, Maureen murmured to herself as she took the lead in her excitement to see what lay beyond the front door.

She grasped hold of Colleen's hand and shook it in a firm, I'm a serious buyer-like manner before stepping aside so as Donal could do the same.

'Now then,' said Agent Colleen. 'I'll show you around first and then leave you both to have a wander at leisure. How does that sound?'

'Grand,' Maureen and Donal murmured as she took off at a canter.

For a sturdy woman she was setting a fair pace, Maureen thought, puffing as she listened to Colleen's spiel about how the house had only recently been converted. The other two mews had been sold off as they were completed to two perfectly lovely couples. A retired couple like themselves and a young professional couple.' She'd whinnied or laughed then, Maureen wasn't sure, as she added, 'So you won't have any worries with the neighbours having wild parties or the like.'

Maureen and Donal looked at one another and managed a titter to humour her.

Satisfied, she continued telling them about the house. It was the last of the three to hit the market and, Colleen added with a hint of urgency in her voice, she'd had a lot of interest. It would sell quickly.

Maureen drew breath, about to say she'd make an offer when she felt the voice of reason, Donal, squeeze her hand reining her in. She zipped her mouth closed and inspected the master bedroom.

Oh, but the house was lovely from what they'd seen so far and this room was gorgeous, Maureen thought, taking in the soft, tasteful grey palette. The walls were painted in a new colour called sea mist, Agent Colleen informed them, as Maureen's feet sank into the plush pile.

There was something deliciously decadent about new carpet she thought, itching to toss her shoes aside and caress the woollen loops. Actually, she wanted to lie down and roll about on it but knew it wouldn't suit her serious buyer persona. Instead, she did a few lunges, throwing in a gentle back bend for good measure.

'Maureen, I have to say I've been admiring those trousers of yours since you arrived. They look very smart and comfortable, so.'

'They're the most versatile item in my wardrobe, Colleen. May I call you Colleen?'

'Please do.'

'These here,' Maureen plucked at the soft fabric, 'are the Mo-pant original.'

Colleen frowned, 'I can't say I've heard of them, Maureen. Are they advertised on the television? You know in one of those late-night shouty, ring this number now adverts?'

'Not at all, Colleen. The Mo-pant is far too exclusive for the likes of that.'

'I wouldn't mind a pair of those myself.' Colleen tugged at her suit jacket, the buttons in danger of popping off and wriggled in her tight trousers. 'To be honest, Maureen, I'm terrified if I bend over in these I'll have the arse out of them. But I'm on the Weight Watchers so I refuse to buy a bigger pair.'

Maureen made a dismissive noise somewhere between a snort and a kind of pooh-poohing sound. 'Been there, done that, worn the trousers, Colleen. I'm hearing you.' She was on a roll, she thought to herself. A natural saleswoman.

Donal, lurking by the curtains, thought she sounded a little like one of the evangelical preachers they'd seen on the television when they'd been on their holidays in Los Angeles.

'Get yerself a pair of these, Colleen, and I promise they'll save you money in the long run.'

Colleen was a shrewd woman and this had her aquiver. 'How so, Maureen?'

'You won't be worried about doing the Weight Watchers anymore because you won't need to. You'll be comfortable in your own skin because that's what these are like, you know, wearing a second skin.' She did a quick lunge to cement her point.

'In fact, there are days I'm out and about I have to stop to check I remembered to put trousers on because I could just as easily be walking about in my knickers. They're that comfortable.'

Colleen was just about salivating now. 'And there's no zips to pinch the tummy roll?'

Maureen pulled the elasticated waistband out. 'Not a zip in sight. They're a one size fits all wonder.' Ooh, she liked that. She'd have to remember that one.

'And where can I buy them, Maureen?'

'Well now, you're in luck. I've just had a shipment arrive direct from London.'

'I'll take five pairs.'

'Done.'

They shook on the deal before Colleen, desperate to get home and take her too tight trousers off, showed them the pièce de résistance, the living room with its entertainer's kitchen off to the side. It overlooked the rectangular clipped stretch of lawn but it was what lay beyond that that would sell the property.

It was as though someone had hung a painting at the bottom of the garden of a glorious stretch of azure water. The bobbing white masts of the yachts punctuating the blue were pootling about in the harbour. It was a moving watercolour.

Maureen gasped and grasped hold of Donal's arm once more.

Colleen was pleased. She was sensing a deal was in the bag. It needed to be. Sales had been down lately and she'd five pairs of Mo-pants to pay for.

'Magnificent, isn't it?'

Donal tried to look non-plussed because he'd been around the block a few times. He knew how these estate agents worked. If this Colleen woman thought they were smitten with the property, she'd push for all she could get. She was working for the vendor, after all, not them.

Maureen however with her whispered mantra of, 'Oh, Donal, I just love it,' was giving the game away.

'Shall I leave you to chat amongst yourselves?'

Donal took charge, 'Yes please, Colleen. Thank you.'

Once she'd disappeared he shook Maureen, 'Earth to Maureen.'

'Oh, Donal, I just love it.'

'I could see us here right enough,' he agreed.

Maureen couldn't tear her eyes away from the view. She was visualising Pooh frolicking on the grass as she and Donal sat hand in hand on the sofa watching the everchanging vista.

Wasn't it funny the way life worked? she thought.

When she'd lost Brian, her life as she'd known it had had to change if she was to carry on and so she'd gone for a sea change and tried apartment living here in Howth.

Her apartment was low maintenance which she'd deemed important for a woman now on her own. The downside of low maintenance meant she'd lots of time on her hands. Maureen wasn't one to sit back and moan and so she'd thrown herself into every activity on offer in the seaside village. Of late, however, she'd had to cut back on a few things or she'd never see Donal.

She still enjoyed the odd ramble, although her casty foot had put paid to that this last while, and she planned on resuming her sailing lessons too. She'd had to pass the baton of her secretarial role on the Keep Howth Beautiful committee to Marjorie Murphy and once she'd finished her latest painting she'd given up her art classes. There wasn't much spare time for golf anymore either. Of course, she and Donal could have played but she'd sensed that might not be good for their relationship. She found it very hard to compromise when it came to competitive sport.

Who'd have thought at her time of life she'd have found love again and be making another move, to a house no less! With a sea view and a garden. A love nest for her and her Donal.

Donal gazed at Maureen with fond exasperation. He was about to launch into his money talk. They'd been to the bank manager and they knew what their top dollar was, taking into account the sale of both Maureen's apartment and his house. They'd agreed they didn't want to pay over and above it because they didn't want to take on any debt. They wanted the freedom to enjoy their life together without financial commitments hovering over their heads.

He sighed and draped an arm around Maureen. He'd a feeling none of that mattered anymore. This was where they belonged and all he could hope was that the price would be right because he'd have a hard time getting Maureen to walk away from it if it wasn't.

Chapter Fifteen

A isling put the phone down, frowning. Moira wasn't answering. She'd tried her twice now and gotten no answer. Either she was still sleeping or she'd left Mammy's and was on her way home or goodness knows where. She wouldn't fret though because Moira was a big girl perfectly able for looking after herself. The most likely scenario was she was on her way to patch things up with Tom and this family conference business would be cancelled. A storm in a teacup so to speak.

It was the not knowing what was going on which was frustrating though, and now she was annoyed at not only Quinn but also Mammy, and as Moira was at the root of whatever had Mammy riled she threw her into the mix too.

She'd no time to dwell on any of this though because she needed to show her face downstairs. She'd a job to do.

Despite her best efforts with her makeup and hair, she felt frazzled and it showed. She took a moment to inhale and exhale slowly a few times, the way Rosi had shown her, hoping it would shake off the cloak of irritation she was wearing. It didn't, and she thudded down the stairs like Big Foot in heels.

Had Tom cheated on Moira? Was that it? Because, yes that would be worthy of a family conference. The O'Mara women would close ranks and call him lots of no-good cheating fecker names. Mammy would probably take advantage of the situation and sing a country music song because they were always on about cheatin' men in country music songs.

There was no denying Tom had a very good bottom on him. It would tempt even the most chaste of women and she'd seen the female diners at Quinn's admiring it, food forgotten as they ogled his undulating cheeks working the room. Mind you, it was hard to imagine him being unfaithful to her sister because he only had eyes for her. Pathetically so. In fact, Aisling fancied, Cindy Crawford could dance around him drinking the Coca-Cola in her red bathers and he'd not blink an eye so maybe it was the other way around.

Hmm, was it Moira who'd been doing the cheating? she pondered as she reached the first-floor landing. She couldn't picture this scenario either. Moira adored Tom more than she adored herself and that was saying something.

She chewed her bottom lip as she breezed into reception to see how James was getting on. It was all very frustrating the not knowing and she'd have to wait hours to find out what was going on now unless Moira put in an appearance before Mammy's conference kicked off. There would be crisps and crackers and dips too she resolved, despite what Mammy had said, because if she had to suffer through the thing she would do so with snacks to hand.

James was checking-in a guest and Aisling mustered up a smile as her professional persona pushed the family drama to one side.

'Good morning,' she said to their young weekend receptionist, noting the empty plate on the desk which signalled Mrs Baicu had made sure he'd had a hearty breakfast. She was very fond of James was Mrs Baicu. From Romania originally, she'd learned to cook a mean full Irish and as the mother of sons, she liked to keep their young weekend helper plied with food.

'Good morning, Aisling, this is, erm, Jennifer Rushmore,' James stuttered his face mottled with patches of red. There was a smudge of bacon grease on his chin.

Aisling turned to welcome their rather stunning guest. She was the sort of woman who instantly made other mere mortal females feel dumpy and dour, especially when they'd been feeling frazzled in the first place. She looked very familiar too, she mused. She must have stayed here before because hers was a face you wouldn't easily forget.

Oh, what she'd give for cheekbones like that, Aisling thought, staring enviously as she fought hard not to suck her cheeks in. This, she knew, didn't make her look like a supermodel but instead resemble a flying lemur, at least according to Moira. She'd been watching a nature programme at the time when Aisling had pulled this face before nudging her to ask whether she could see her cheekbones. The creature on the screen, Moira said she took after, was all googly eyes and pointy chin and as such she'd stopped doing the sucky-in face immediately.

So, it was with this in mind, Aisling, remembering herself, stopped staring and gave a gracious hostess smile. 'Hello there, I'm Aisling O'Mara, welcome to O'Mara's.'

It was apparent James thought their guest was something special too because he'd do well to close his mouth she thought with a sideways glance.

'Thank you and call me Jennifer, please.'

Her accent was softly American and Patrick and Cindy would kill for that smile, Aisling thought, almost as dazzled as James. Speaking of whom, she gave him a pointed look and he stopped drooling long enough to retrieve the key for the room from the pigeon holes behind him.

She was in Room 10, Aisling saw, surprised. It was their largest room. O'Mara's version of a penthouse suite with glorious views over the Green. It was a very big space just for one.

'How long will you be staying with us, Jennifer?'

'Five nights. I'd like to stay longer and explore Ireland but I've commitments back home.'

'Where abouts in the States are you from?' Aisling asked politely.

'I'm a southern girl but I live in Malibu these days.'

Aisling was away then, telling Jennifer Rushmore all about the family's recent holiday to Los Angeles. She left out the part where they'd all been running around her uncle Cormac's mansion in their nightwear being terrorised by a racoon but she did tell her how much she'd enjoyed the *It's a Small World* ride at Disneyland.

Jennifer stood listening politely and when Aisling finally stopped to draw breath she asked, 'I don't suppose you'd know of anywhere low-key for dinner tonight? Somewhere with a traditional vibe would be nice.'

'As it happens I know just the place.' Aisling retrieved one of Quinn's brochures which Jennifer glanced over.

'It looks very Irish and exactly what I had in mind.' She bestowed a full wattage beam on Aisling who basked in it.

'Grand, I can make a reservation for you if you like?'

'It's not too short a notice for Saturday night?'

'Normally, yes, but because I'm married to the owner, no. I'll make sure you get a table. Will you be dining alone?'

Jennifer flushed in a way that became her but would have had Aisling looking like a beetroot. 'No, there's two of us.'

'No problem. Would seven thirty suit you?'

'That would be great, thank you so much.'

They'd very good manners the Americans, Aisling always thought. They used their pleases and thank yous liberally. 'You're welcome and if there's anything else you'd like to see or do while you're here we're only too happy to help.' She would not be recommending Dublin's latest Viking boat tour that was for sure. 'Oh, and before I forget, breakfast is still being served in the dining room downstairs and there's tea and coffee available in the guest lounge.' She did her flight attendant arm demonstration.

James came around from behind the desk to pick up their guest's enormous suitcase. 'I'll take your bag up to your room, Miss, erm, Jennifer.'

'Thank you, honey. You're a sweetheart,' she drawled.

James went even redder and hefting the case, he set off up the stairs bounding like an eager puppy despite the weight of the case he was dragging behind him.

Jennifer made to follow him but Aisling had to ask, 'Have you stayed with us before, Jennifer? I never forget a face and you seem very familiar.'

The younger woman donned a coy expression. 'No, I have one of those faces I think. This is my first time in Ireland.'

'Oh!' Aisling was perplexed, she could have sworn they'd met before. 'Well then, we've turned it on for you today with the blue sky. I hope you enjoy your stay.'

Jennifer smiled her gratitude and Aisling couldn't help but feel she'd been bestowed with a special gift. She wondered what it would be like to have that sort of effect on people as she watched Jennifer Rushmore take to the stairs. She wondered too what it would be like to make plain old jeans and a shirt look like they had just stepped off the Paris runways. She'd look like she was in the middle of doing DIY in the same attire.

Ah well, the world would be a dull place if we were all supermodels, Aisling told herself, spying a few petals that had fallen from the bouquet on top of the front desk. She plucked them up and dropped them into the wastepaper basket under the desk. A fresh bouquet was due to arrive on Monday and she titivated the blooms that were only now beginning to fade before picking up the empty breakfast plate. She was about to take it down to the kitchen and see how Mrs Baicu was getting on when James reappeared.

He was fidgety with excitement Aisling noticed, wondering at the effect a pretty face had on him. It was a shame he didn't pay attention to a girl closer to his own age who happened to take over his shift at four pm.

'Aisling, do you know who that was?' he half whispered.

'Yes, Jennifer Rushmore. She seemed very nice.'

'No, not Jennifer Rushmore.' He shook his head like a dog would after frolicking out of the sea. 'That was Jenny Seymour.'

Aisling stared at him. Then her mouth fell open, mirroring James' earlier expression. 'As in Jenny Seymour from my all-time favourite sitcom, *The Apartment?*' He was right, she realised. She knew she'd seen her somewhere, she just hadn't twigged it had been on the tele. She'd been so upset when they'd canned the series but Jenny Seymour's career had taken off in the aftermath.

'She must be here to promote her new film, *Here We Go Again*,' James said. 'It's not my sort of thing but my sister's keen to see it, mostly because it's got Jackson Creed in it.'

'It's being billed as *Bridget Jones* meets *The Runaway Bride*,' Aisling said, having read about it in a magazine when she was waiting to see the doctor the other week. She quite fancied seeing it herself but knew she'd have to rally up Leila to go with her because Quinn would have no interest, besides which he was in her bad books.

She'd not told Quinn she'd gone to the doctors. A part of her had known what Dr Lewisham would tell her; that it was far too early to be worrying about exploring the various fertility options available for couples having trouble conceiving and that she needed to take a deep breath and calm down.

She didn't know why she was so tied in knots about this baby-making business. The only thing she could put it down to was fear. The fear of not being able to have something she so desperately wanted for her and Quinn. She was thirty-seven and it was a fact that women's fertility went down rapidly with each passing year after thirty-five.

To be fair Dr Lewisham had been very kind and she'd not said Aisling was neurotic but had suggested she eat plenty of leafy greens and that she should think about taking a vitamin B supplement. She'd reached over and patted her on the hand and said she'd be grand if she relaxed about it all and she was sure Aisling would be back to see her with the good news she was expecting in no time at all.

Aisling had stopped at the Tesco's on the way home and bought an enormous bunch of kale. She didn't even like the stuff.

James intruded on her thoughts. 'I can't wait to tell my pals we've a Hollywood star staying here at O'Mara's.'

Aisling was assailed with a mental image of a reception area filled with hormonal young lads, loitering in the hope of a glimpse of their famous guest. No, it wouldn't do.

'You can't tell anyone she's here, James.'

He looked crestfallen.

'She's booked under a false name to throw the press off I'd say. She obviously doesn't want it made public knowledge she's staying here. If she'd wanted to be snapped every time she stepped out the doors she'd have opted for The Shelbourne or The Clarence.' The bigger hotels were places to be seen, unlike their guesthouse which, while charming, didn't have the celebrity pull or glitz of the other two.

James' shoulders slumped. Jenny Seymour was staying at the guesthouse where he worked, where nothing all that exciting ever happened, and he couldn't say anything. Life could be very unfair at times. Aisling was right though, he supposed and, he thought, remembering the crisp note she'd pressed into his hand, she was a good tipper. The least he could do was respect her privacy.

The door opened then and a blond-haired man wearing dark glasses and a furtive expression stepped inside. He closed the door behind him and waited a beat as though expecting someone to burst through it.

'Hello there,' Aisling called out cheerily, thinking they'd a right one here.

The man turned away from the door and moved towards reception, pushing his glasses up into the thick thatch of wheaten hair in order to fix Aisling with his piercingly blue eyes. Her breath caught in her throat, he was a living breathing Adonis and there was something very familiar about him, she thought, with a sense of déja vu.

His broad shoulders relaxed under his fitted shirt as he mustered up a warm smile to reveal a dimple in his left cheek that made her knees go weak. He was as handsome as Jenny Seymour was beautiful. The Ken to her Barbie.

'Hey there.' He'd an American twang too and James was goggly eyed once more.

Where'd she seen him before? Aisling asked herself.

'You've a guest staying with you under the name of Jennifer Rushmore, could you tell her that uh, John Smith is here to see her.'

Aisling's eyes widened. They weren't very good at this false name business, she thought, gazing into the swoon-worthy eyes of Jackson Creed, Hollywood heart-throb. She momentarily forgot she was a married woman with an axe to grind with her husband as she soaked in his manliness.

An amused smile played at the corner of his mouth and Aisling deduced he was used to the effect he had on women. She was also in danger of dribbling and, dragging her eyes away reluctantly, she rang through to Room 10 and told their incognito movie star guest that a John Smith was waiting in reception for her.

James and Aisling looked up as the skipping light tread on the stairs reached reception. It was like watching a scene from their new film as a radiant Jenny or Jennifer appeared and John or Jackson's face shone with naked adoration. Both James and Aisling wished they had hearing on a par with Maureen's as the golden couple briefly retreated to the privacy of the guest lounge before taking to the stairs at a rate of knots that suggested there'd be shenanigans going on in Room 10 before too long.

Aisling turned to James who seemed to know what was what in Hollywood. 'I thought Jackson Creed was—'

'Married, to Ellie Ashmore.' He nodded and they both raised their eyes upwards wondering if his wife and fellow actress was aware her husband was currently alone with Jenny Seymour in Room 10 of O'Mara's Guesthouse on the Green.

Chapter Sixteen

The shock of realising a scandalous affair was underway at the guesthouse reaffirmed Aisling's earlier resolution that she must have crisps. So, keen to sniff the fresh air after the day she'd had so far, she trotted off down to the Baggot Street Tesco.

There'd been no further sighting of their celebrity guests which was probably just as well because she wouldn't know where to put herself when they eventually did emerge. And, they'd have to appear eventually because she'd made their dinner reservation as requested by Ms Rushmore aka Seymour.

The thought of the field day the press would have if they knew what was going on at O'Mara's between the stars of the latest Hollywood blockbuster made her shudder. It wasn't as if they'd a back exit the duo could use to slip out undetected if anyone did let the cat out of the bag, not unless they wanted to scale the wall to the Iveagh Gardens where Mr Fox lived.

It was a good job she trusted their staff to be discreet, Aisling told herself as she rounded the corner into her favourite aisle in the supermarket. The one filled with salty, crunchy gorgeousness.

Quinn had yet to return from golf when she'd left O'Mara's and as such, she threw an extra bag in her basket knowing only the kettle fried barbecue flavoured ones would have the magical powers to soothe her.

As she paid for the items, she wondered if Moira was home yet and what Mammy would do if she'd gone missing in action. It was all very mysterious whatever it was going on, but at least she'd be put out of her misery in an hour and the adulterous affair being carried out in Room 10 had at least proved a distraction.

She returned to the guesthouse to find James in earnest conversation with young Evie, a fellow student who manned the front desk of an evening at the weekend. Aisling often marvelled at how dense the opposite sex could be at times. It was clear to her that Evie had a crush on James who, if she were twenty years younger, she'd deem crushworthy too.

Was James aware of this? No, he'd no clue, and Evie was a lovely girl; he could do a lot worse than her. She knew she was going to have to play matchmaker as she had with Bronagh and Leonard Walsh if they didn't sort themselves out soon.

Now though, Aisling knew exactly what the topic of conversation would be.

'Hello there, Evie.'

'Aisling! James is after telling me who's upstairs.' Her eyes were bugging with the drama of it all. 'Can you believe it?'

No, actually, she was having a very hard time believing it but as the manager of the guesthouse, it was up to her to ensure her staff respected their guests' privacy and so she had to play spoilsport. 'It was certainly unexpected, Evie, but as I told James earlier, we owe it to our guests to keep their comings and goings private. Do you understand?' She smiled to soften her words.

Evie's shoulders drooped. She'd planned to get on the telephone to all her friends with the breaking news James had just relayed, once Aisling had gone upstairs.

It was very disappointing being told she was expected to be discreet. She enjoyed her job here at O'Mara's though, particularly because she got to see James every weekend and as such, she'd respect what she been told. She nodded and James, finding himself pinned under Aisling's gaze, did the same.

She looked from one to the other and, satisfied she'd made her point, she hauled her groceries upstairs. Her gaze flitted down the corridor when she reached the floor Room 10 was situated on but the door was firmly closed and she found herself penning one of her Dear Aisling letters as she stood poised with her hand resting lightly on the bannister.

Dear Aisling,

I run a respectable and well-loved guesthouse in Dublin. However, I'm worried the reputation of our hotel and my family name will change as I've a guest staying who's a famous American actress. She's here to promote her new film and she's after having an affair with her co-star who happens to be married and always putting on PDAs with his wife for the magazines. Yer woman's obviously chosen our guesthouse for her clandestine meetings because it will be easier for them to come and go undetected. I'm worried that it will get out though because these things always do and our guesthouse will make the papers for all the wrong reasons. They're a couple who're playing with fire and I've a feeling in my water it's not going to end well for them or us.

What should I do?

Yours faithfully,

Me

She answered herself. There's nothing you can do, Aisling, it's none of your business and you should be worrying about yourself saying things like you can feel it in your water. You're turning into Mammy. With that, she carried on up the final flight of stairs.

'Hello!' she called out, pushing open the apartment door in case Moira was back.

'In here, love,' Quinn called back.

Aisling's eyes narrowed. The wanderer had returned. She found him on the sofa scribbling in a notebook with the football playing on mute on the television in the background. Her nose detected he'd not long polished off a cheese toastie and a stab of unreasonable resentment that he'd not made one for her too shot through her.

Quinn looked up from what he was doing, trying to gauge his wife's mood and, spying the numerous bags of crisps she was unloading onto the kitchen worktop, he decided it wasn't good.

'How's your day been, Ash?' He injected a cheery note into his voice. 'I stopped off at Mam and Dad's after golf. She'd been baking. There's a container of her ginger biscuits there for you because she knows how you love them and I made you a cheese toastie in case you were hungry. It's in the oven, it'll still be warm if you eat it now.'

The kind gestures on his mam's part and his after she'd been thinking such mean thoughts saw her blink back guilty tears. This was hopeless, it was time to be honest. 'Quinn, did you stay late at work last night and go to golf first thing,' she sniffed, 'to avoid me?' She'd not planned on saying anything but carrying around all these festering worries wasn't doing either of them any good.

'What?' Quinn stared over at her.

'You heard.' She ripped a piece of paper towel off the roll and blew her nose noisily.

Quinn closed the book he'd been jotting new menu ideas down in and made his way to the kitchen. He pulled Aisling to him and she put her head on his chest, breathing in his familiar scent greedily. She didn't want to be at odds with him. She hated it when things weren't right between them.

'No, well yeah, kind of.' He sighed. 'Yes, alright, I *was* avoiding you and not because I don't love you,' he said, refusing to loosen his embrace as she looked up at him with tears clinging to her lashes. 'I love you, Ash, you know that, but you've been so intense since we started trying for a family. I've been feeling like one of those performing bears dancing to your tune.'

Aisling spluttered. 'Quinn Moran, you're full of yerself so you are, bear indeed.'

He grinned. 'Donkey then.'

She slapped at him playfully but knew the point he was trying to make was genuine. 'I'm sorry I've been at you all the time. I'm just scared. I mean what if it doesn't happen for us?'

'Why wouldn't it?' Quinn frowned.

'I don't know. It's one of those things though, isn't it? You take it for granted that when you decide to start a family it'll happen but it doesn't, not for everybody.' She sniffed but also felt a great unburdening as she told him how she'd been feeling. She also wanted the cheese toastie. She disengaged herself from him and retrieved the plate from the oven. Biting into the toasted sandwich it oozed cheese out the side. Nobody made a cheese toastie better than her husband. 'Thank you,' she mumbled through her mouthful.

He grinned watching her. He loved the way she enjoyed her food although she was chewing a bit manically and as such he chose his words carefully. 'Well, I suppose if it didn't happen for us we'd look into other avenues but whatever happens, Ash, I promise you we'll face it together. We're a team remember?'

She nodded, making short work of the sandwich, 'And I promise I won't be at you about the riding every five minutes.'

Maureen appeared at that moment and told Aisling not to be talking with her mouthful while Moira, swaggering in a manner that told Aisling she was in the poo because she always adopted her cock of the walk swagger when she was for it, said, 'Thank the Lord for small mercies like me having a break from listening to the pair of you making the headboard bang.'

'Moira, don't be talking like that in front of Donal!' Maureen turned and mouthed 'sorry' at Donal who was hovering in the doorway to the living room.

He just shrugged, well used to the O'Mara women and their carry on since he'd spent ten days in Los Angeles with them all. Still and all, he was glad Quinn was here, he'd have been a little frightened if he were to be the only male present at this family conference Maureen was after scheduling. She'd insisted he come because (a) he was family and (b) they'd a happy announcement of their own to be making.

Aisling glanced at the clock. It was one minute to four. 'Quinn, I haven't had a chance to tell you but Mammy's after organising a family conference. It's something to do with Moira.'

Moira scowled at her sister.

Meanwhile, Maureen had bustled into the kitchen and taken a spoon from the drawer. She picked up a glass draining on the worktop and began tapping the side of it to get their attention. The family conference was about to begin.

Chapter Seventeen

'Right then, before we start, does anyone need the toilet?' Maureen asked, her eyes sweeping over the faces dotted about the room. 'Because now's the time to go if you do.'

Aisling sighed. 'Mammy you used to say that when we were little. We're all adults here now. Perfectly able to decide when we need the toilet, thanks very much.'

'If I put my hand up during the family conference because I need a wee will I be allowed to go?' Moira asked.

'No,' Maureen shot back at Moira before glaring at Aisling. 'Says she who used to stamp her foot and say she'd wet her knickers if she didn't get to the toilet every single time we were on a family outing. A nightmare you were. What do you say to that, Aisling O'Mara?'

'Moran-O'Mara,' Aisling corrected, feeling the love for her husband once more as she smiled at him. Unfortunately, she'd cheese dangling from her chin. Good husband that he was, Quinn wiped it off.

'She always was a messy eater,' Maureen tutted. 'And do you know, Quinn, I could set my watch by her when she was small. We'd get five minutes down the road and she'd start moaning on about needing the toilet.' She shook her head at the memory.

'She still does that.' Quinn sidestepped Aisling's swipe, grinning. Then, seeing Maureen had turned her attention to ensuring Donal was seated comfortably he made to slink from the room. There was no need for him to be part of this round the table chat about whatever it was Moira had been up to.

'Stop right there, Quinn Moran-O'Mara.' Maureen held her hand up like a Spice Girl.

'It's only me with the double-barrelled name, Mammy,' Aisling interjected.

Maureen ignored her. 'You're a part of this family too, so sit down.' She gestured to the seat on her left where she could keep an eye on him.

Quinn did as he was told.

Maureen turned her attention back to Donal who'd picked up the salt shaker and was toying with it. She gave his hand a gentle slap. 'Donal, it's bad luck to be spilling the salt. Don't be tempting fate.'

He dutifully put the shaker down and looked over at Quinn. They exchanged a moment of silent male bonding over what they were about to endure.

'Aisling, would you get your hand out of the crisp packet and fetch the telephone. I'll ring Pat on that and Moira can ring Rosi on her mobile. I've worked out the time difference and we should be grand to get hold of him.'

Aisling wiped her salty fingers on the tea towel before tipping the rest of the bag into a bowl. She carried the crisps and the phone over to the table and sat down next to her sister eyeing her suspiciously.

'Mammy, tell her to stop staring at me,' Moira said, arms folded across her chest as she slumped in her seat. 'She's giving me the evil eye, so.'

'Shush, Moira, and call Rosi.' Maureen shifted importantly in her chair. She'd have liked to have been a judge. She'd have been very good at it. Fair and just, she thought.

Moira fumbled around in her bag for her mobile. She was in no mood for this impromptu get-together. Her head was woolly because she'd slept late. She'd woken after eleven thanks to the telephone ringing and ringing. She'd decided to ignore it seeing O'Mara's on the caller display and guessing it was Aisling.

A large note had been propped next to the kettle to say Mammy and Donal had gone to look at a house. Mammy had also underlined that she was to telephone Tom and sort things out. She hadn't.

Instead, she'd nursed a cup of tea, wishing Mammy was there to make her toast because toast always tasted better when someone else made it for you.

She'd mulled over how badly things had gone with Tom the night before until she was thoroughly sick of herself and had given in to Pooh's wheedling, taking him for a walk down the pier. The sea air had done little to blow away the awful sick feeling she had whenever she thought about what Tom had said and she'd had a moment of panic when she'd spotted someone with a walking pole in the distance but it wasn't Rosemary. She wondered if it were a Howth thing, the walking pole.

It should be him ringing her, apologising for the way he'd reacted she'd decided, returning to the apartment and putting on some maudlin country music partly for Pooh and partly so as she could wallow in her misery.

She'd checked her mobile every five minutes just in case she'd somehow missed his call and when Mammy and Donal had returned all skittish and annoyingly happy they'd found her sobbing to Willy Nelson's Blue Eyes Crying in the Rain.

Now, with her mobile pressed to her ear she hit speed dial for Rosi's number. As across the table, Mammy was shouting about what the country code for Los Angeles was.

She listened to it ring and ring and glanced up hopefully. Rosi wasn't home. It wouldn't be fair to have a family conference without her. She was just about to tell this to Mammy when her sister's breathless voice sounded down the line.

'Rosi, it's me, Moira,' she said glumly as Mammy, having been supplied the code by Donal announced, 'It's ringing.' Mammy pointed to the telephone she held in her hand to make sure no one was confused as to what she meant.

Moira listened as Roisin said, 'Can I call you back, Moira? You haven't rung at a good time. Shay's here and Noah's out with his dad.'

Moira met her mammy's eye across the table, 'Rosi's after doing the riding with Shay because Noah's out with his dad, Mammy. She wants to know can she call us back?'

They all heard Rosi's tinny voice shrieking from the mobile as she told her sister to shut up.

Maureen meanwhile turned purple as she shouted across the table, 'I've had it up to here with the riding talk. The riding tis the reason we're all sitting here now! Oh, hello there, Cindy, it's Maureen.' She pulled a face hearing her firstborn's partner gush, 'Oh hi, Mom!'

'Er, hello there yourself, Cindy. Is Patrick about? Because we're after having a family conference.' She put her hand over the receiver. 'She's after picking up the extension because she says she's family too.'

She pulled a face, still not having come to terms with Cindy as the perfect match for her beloved Pat but then was all smiles hearing his voice come on the line. 'Patrick, it's your mammy calling.'

All eyes around the table chose that moment to swing toward Moira wondering why'd they'd been summoned and what she'd done. Moira slunk further down in her seat.

What's going on? Aisling asked.Nobody answered.

Maureen was the next to speak. 'Can you hear if I hold the phone out like so, Pat? You can too, Cindy?' She pulled a face once more but said, 'Grand, because we're gathered here today—'

'Mammy, it's not a fecking wedding service.' Moira had had enough. 'I'm pregnant, everybody.' She hurled this into the phone she had in her hand dropping it down on the table before leaning over to the receiver Mammy was holding out toward her to spell it out, 'p.r.e.g.n.a.n.t! And Tom's after telling me he doesn't want a baby. So, I'm to be a solo mammy. There, now you have it.' Moira burst into noisy tears.

Aisling's first instinct was to put her arm around her sister but she was too taken aback by what she'd just announced. She stared at Moira's pinched face, which was blotchy with tears, wanting to comfort her, but a lump was beginning to form in her own throat and she couldn't move. How could Moira be pregnant? She should be the one who was announcing she was expecting.

Roisin was shouting out from the mobile demanding someone pick up and explain exactly what was going on.

Aisling sat there trying to swallow the lump but it was growing bigger as her sister's revelation sank in. Then, feeling as though she couldn't breathe, she pushed her chair back and ran from the room not wanting anyone to see her tears. It was all too much, she thought, putting distance between herself and her family as she slammed the bedroom door behind her.

Quinn watched her go and got up, pausing before pushing his chair back in. 'Erm, congratulations, Moira,' he offered up uncertainly before heading off to check on his wife.

Donal was the next to move. 'I'll make us a nice cup of tea.'

Maureen nodded as she put the phone to her ear once more, 'I'll call you back when everyone's calmed down, Pat. Yes, yes, a baby, yes Moira, I know.'

She did the same with Rosi as she squinted at the small device trying to find an off button.

'I told you a family conference was a stupid idea, Mammy,' Moira sniffed, pulling a tissue from the box Donal was holding out to her. She blew her nose, shoving the tissue up her sleeve before flouncing off to her room.

Maureen didn't say anything. She'd thought they'd all be like your Waltons ones or your lovely Michael J Fox sitcom that used to be on the tele years ago. They'd talk it all through and Moira would feel blessed to know she'd a loving supportive family behind her.

Instead, it had played out like a scene from the *Addams Family* and she'd not even had the chance to share her and Donal's exciting news about the house. It was all very disappointing.

Chapter Eighteen

'There's no point in us hanging around here any longer, Donal,' Maureen said, having finished her tea. She'd rung both Roisin and Patrick back to confirm that yes, Moira was pregnant and yes, Aisling had her nose out of joint given she and Quinn were wanting to start a family themselves. Oh, and yes, both girls were holed up in their bedrooms with faces on them that would curdle the milk. And, no it would take more than a packet of Snowballs to fix things.

When they'd stopped exclaiming over the family bombshell, she'd managed to drop in her and Donal's exciting news. The news however of the offer they'd made that morning on their dream house overlooking the sea fell rather flat after all the drama of the other. The wind had gone out of Maureen's sails with a big whoosh. There was no point gushing about it when she didn't have a rapt audience.

Yes, she mused again, picking her and Donal's empty cups up and carrying them over to the sink, it was all very disappointing.

Quinn had reappeared while she'd been in conversation with Patrick and he'd chatted with Donal out of earshot until Maureen had gotten off the telephone. Now he turned his focus to Maureen.

'I think it's Ash's hormones has her behaving like so, Maureen. She's all over the show lately,' he offered up lamely. 'I'll leave her be for a while.'

'She's never been any different, Quinn. She's very single-minded is Aisling, sets her heart on something and that's all she can think about. She'll come right and if she's not out of her room in an hour you could try frying some bacon, that usually has her come running,' Maureen soothed.

She also knew from experience when her girls stomped off to their bedrooms it was the best place for them. Give them a few hours to cool off and they'd be grand. Or, at least she hoped they would. They were in unchartered waters. 'Anyway, we'll leave you to it.'

Quinn looked as though he'd very much not like to be left to it.

'Pooh will be desperate for a walk,' Maureen added, reading his expression.

'Fair play,' he sighed and then remembering what Donal had told him said, 'Oh and congratulations on the new house. I'm sure Aisling will be made up for you.'

'Thank you.' She gave her son-in-a-law a squeeze and pat on the back then, feeling rather like she was leaving him aboard a sinking ship, she and Donal took to the stairs.

When they reached reception there was no sign of James manning the front desk and perturbed, Maureen poked her head around the door to the guests' lounge. She spotted him with his nose glued to the window.

'What are you gawping at there, James?'

James jumped and turned away from whatever had grabbed his attention to address Maureen, his face anxious. 'Oh howya, Mrs O'Mara? I was about to ring upstairs to ask Aisling to come down. I'm not sure what to do. I told them they're trespassing if they try to come inside.'

'Who's after wanting to trespass?' Maureen asked, bustling over to the window to see what was going on. There was a huddle of men and women of mixed ages all powwowing on the pavement outside.

'Who're all those people jostling about out there? Donal come and see?'

Donal dutifully trooped over and squeezed in next to Maureen for a look.

'I think they're paps, Mrs O'Mara,' James supplied.

'Paps?' She frowned. 'Is that like the Jehovah's Witness or Morons? They get about in groups like so, doing the door knocking to spread the word. They mean well enough but there's an awful lot of them out there come to convert us.'

'Mormons, Maureen,' Donal corrected. 'And they're usually much more smartly dressed.'

'With bicycles,' James added. 'And paps is short for paparazzi.'

'Like yer wans that tormented the poor Princess Diana?'

James nodded. 'Yeah, I think they're here because of you know who upstairs.'

'Jaysus wept, what's Moira after doing now! As if being collared on suspicion of shoplifting a pregnancy testing kit wasn't bad enough. Donal, I don't think my poor old heart can take much more!'

James stared at Maureen as though she'd just flown down from Mars.

Donal took charge. 'Now then, Maureen, deep breaths, that's it. James, what are you talking about?'

'I thought Aisling would have told you. Although she did say not to breathe a word but somebody's obviously given them lot out there the heads-up.'

'James!' Maureen demanded wanting him to get to the point.

'Jenny Seymour booked into room ten this morning under a false name and Jackson Creed is up there with her.'

'And who are they when they're at home?' The names meant nothing to Maureen or Donal.

'Erm, they're famous actors from America, Mrs O'Mara.'

'Staying here?' Maureen tried to take it in. She'd had yer man from the BBC here once while he scouted locations in Dublin for a television programme but never an actual celebrity. Besides, there was only one celebrity who'd have her blood racing. She pictured Daniel Day Lewis in his Last of the Mohicans loin cloth ducking into the guests lounge in search of a cup of Earl Grey. Which, she would of course be on hand to make.

'How famous?' she asked coming back to the here and now. 'Are we talking on a par with Rock and Doris? Ingrid and Humphrey, Sonny and Cher?' She couldn't think of any more famous couples but thought she'd given enough examples.

'Who?'

'Never mind, son. They're big names, yes?' Donal said.

James nodded, 'Big, big names.'

'Are they married or is your Jackson one her man friend like,' Maureen asked, hungry for details.

'That's where it gets tricky, Mrs O'Mara. You see Jackson Creed is married, just not to Jenny Seymour.'

'Then what's he doing in her room?' Maureen looked at Donal as though he held the answer.

Donal shrugged. 'Rehearsing?'

'I don't think they're after rehearsing,' James said. 'Aisling and I saw the way they looked at one another. I think that's what has that lot out there hovering.'

Maureen made a tutting noise. 'It's just like Monroe and Kennedy, so. Right here in O'Mara's. And we all know how that ended.' Her eyes narrowed and she glanced out the window once more. 'They could be C&A operatives for all we know.'

'CIA, Maureen,' Donal corrected.

'That's what I said.'

'I don't think it's likely, Mo. James said yer man is a fellow actor not the President of the United States.'

Maureen didn't like being corrected and her tone was terse. 'It's a thin line between acting and politics, Donal.'

Donal decided to let her have the last word. It was why they made such a grand pair. He knew when to say nothing.

'Well, they're blocking the pavement. We can't have this,' Maureen said, flicking a speck of lint off her Mo-pants. She fluffed her hair, wetted her lips, sucked in her tummy, and stalked out to reception. She felt as though she were a magnet being pulled toward the fridge as her feet carried her over to the front door. This was her moment.

She wrenched open the door to the street outside, aware of Donal and James bringing up the rear nervously, no clue as to what she was about to do. Little did they know, she'd no clue as to what she was about to do either.

A cry went up amongst the reporters, and camera shutters whirred and clicked.

Instinct kicked in and Maureen stepped forth. She'd harboured dreams of modelling but was far too short and when she'd had her moment to strut her stuff down the catwalk in Los Angeles she'd fallen off and done her ankle in. Now though, the angels had seen fit to give her a second chance. She took a deep breath and struck a pose because she was a firm believer in second chances.

Chapter Nineteen

Joan

Joan was in a quandary that had her biting her nails, a habit she'd tried to break over the years but had never quite managed to kick into touch.

The reason for this was Gordon, with whom she sat and chatted on her way home from the shops of a Friday.

Friday had rolled around yet again and today she'd sat down, excited to show him the dish that had taken her fancy. There'd been no Toby jugs to be found today but the dish had made up for this. She'd swooped on it and had held it reverently, admiring the elaborate gold edging and delicate violets tied together by a leafy green design. She'd turned it upside down to inspect the stamp with her breath held. Exhaling as her suspicion was confirmed. It was Limoges no less.

It was the sort of dish the queen herself would eat from Gordon had said, taking it from her with a twinkle in his eye. He'd admired its creator's attention to detail before passing it back to Joan. She wrapped it back up in the newspaper as Gordon began to chat about the US Golf Open.

She wasn't much interested in golf but she'd heard of Tiger Woods right enough and she enjoyed their conversation.

Gordon used to play golf he told her but arthritis had stolen that pleasure from him. They'd both agreed aging could be a sod but the alternative was worse and that was when he'd broken ranks and come out with something completely unexpected. An invitation.

He'd asked her to tea. Nothing elaborate he'd stressed but he knew his way around the kitchen right enough. The task of preparing the evening meal had fallen to him when his wife had gotten sick and to his surprise, he'd found he enjoyed cooking. It relaxed him.

He'd be delighted to have her company, he added, because there was no pleasure to be found in cooking for one. Would Friday week suit? That would give him a chance to plan his menu.

Joan hadn't known where to put herself, especially when he spoke of a menu, which clearly pointed to there being more than a sandwich and slice of cake on offer.

Good manners were next to godliness or so her dear late mammy used to say and so Joan had automatically smiled her thanks and said that sounded a grand idea. She'd look forward to it she said, picking up her bag and making her way home, anxious to put distance between herself and Gordon so she could figure out what she should do.

She'd sat amidst the clutter of her front room stewing as to his gesture. Was it done out of kindness, pity? She didn't need the latter but she wasn't averse to the former. Everybody needed kindness in their lives.

She was still stewing now on this, a glorious Saturday, which should have had her full of the joys of the late summer that had come to visit Ireland.

She was wedged into the corner of the old sofa, in the space she managed to keep clear, with a pile of photographs she'd been about to sift through on her lap.

The thing was she thought, turning Gordon's off the cuff invitation over in her mind yet again, she'd gotten used to her daily routine. To eating alone. To being alone. It was the way she lived her life and although she didn't particularly like it, she'd accepted it. She had her routines and Joan didn't like change. Change made her feel unsettled.

She was a creature of habit and if she was the poetic sort then she'd describe the house in which she'd always lived as her cocoon. The detritus she collected and stacked around her kept her safe.

This wasn't against any tangible threat but rather the harshness of the world in general because she knew first-hand what a brutal place it could be. In here though, the world outside ceased to exist and that was the way she liked it.

She rolled her eyes thinking of her brother. She loved Leonard dearly but he'd been a terrible nag each time he came back to Dublin and saw her collection of treasures had grown.

He'd tell her the place smelled unkempt and that Mam and Dad would be ashamed of the way she was living.

'You of all people should know better, Joan,' he'd berated her the last time he'd been here. 'You're living in a death trap. It's a tinder box waiting to go up.'

She'd retorted, 'Lightening doesn't strike twice.' This was untrue of course but the thought of inhabiting this space without her things around her made her throat constrict.

He'd offered to help her clean things up but Joan knew what he really meant was clear the place out. Not everything was precious, she thought, with a guilty glance at the old newspapers piled high about the place but she couldn't bear to part with any of it.

If her bits and pieces were taken away she'd be left exposed. She'd be like a baby bird with no feathers and she couldn't have that.

She turned her attention to the photographs. She'd found them in one of the boxes she'd packed with her parents' belongings after they'd both passed.

It was a low blow on Leonard's part having brought them up like so. She knew full well they'd be upset about the way things were now. Mam had always been a house-proud woman. But that was sort of the point. Mam wasn't here and neither was Dad. It was after they'd passed she'd moved from collecting items she deemed to be treasure to, well, collecting everything. She couldn't bear to throw anything out.

It had been a hard thing to do, to pack away what constituted their parents' lives but she'd set to the task, boxing the things they'd no longer need and which were of no use to her or Leonard. He'd offered to come over and help her but she'd been content to sift through the memories on her own.

She'd held a much-loved scarf of her mam's up, burying her face in the sheer fabric and inhaling the essence of her still clinging to it as if it might bring her back. There was no coming back from death though. When you were gone, you were gone. Things, however, didn't leave you.

She'd sent Leonard their dad's old Kodak Brownie Hawkeye and his leather-strapped watch to have as keepsakes, keeping a few pieces of jewellery belonging to her mam for herself. Leonard had written back, surprised that she'd parted with the camera given the love of photography their dad had passed on to her.

She'd written back she'd no use for it these days and sure, he might as well as keep for it posterity.

She'd fully intended to telephone the thrift shop and ask them to come and collect the boxes once she'd sealed the last of them up but she'd never made the call. She'd been unable to part with them.

She picked up the stack of pictures now. They'd been snapped by her father with his old camera and flicking through them was like looking at a kaleidoscope of the past.

She'd always meant to put the photographs into albums too. They'd hundreds of them with both her and Dad having been keen amateur photographers.

Some days, when she was missing her parents and the way things had once been particularly badly, she'd go and stand at the top of the stairs to the basement to catch a whiff of those peculiar metallic, ammonia fumes. They still clung to the walls of the basement he'd used as his darkroom even now, all these years later. She couldn't stand to go down there any more though. It had been her and Dad's special place. A place where they'd brought images to life as they sifted them back and forth through the solutions before hanging them to dry.

The picture she held came into focus and she shivered despite the warmth of the day. It was of a petite woman in a leotard and had been taken from a distance. She was holding a stick for balance as she stepped out on a tight rope strung high above the sawdust-covered floor of the arena.

The image had been forever frozen in time the day they'd gone to see the circus that had come to Terenure. It was the year Joan had turned sixteen.

She'd been full of restless, teenage stirrings and a trip to the circus had seemed the sort of thing a child would get excited about. She'd behaved like a brat she recalled now. An ungrateful adolescent whose parents had thought they were giving her a lovely day out. In the end, they'd suggested she bring her friend Brigid along for company because Leonard was away at sea having joined the navy by then. Her mood had picked up at the thought of her best pal to link arms with and giggle over secrets no one else would understand.

Despite their studied cool, both girls had been excited by the time they were seated under the big top. You couldn't not be. The anticipation in the excited chatter of the audience clustered in a circle around the ring was infectious.

Joan's father had a field day photographing the different acts. She remembered hearing the click of the camera shutter as she breathed in the foreign scents of animals and roasting peanuts. She knew he was a little hurt that she'd lost interest in what had been their shared hobby of late.

The trapeze artists had been her favourite. She'd watched them fearlessly glide through the air with awe and imagined what it would be like to trust another person to hold onto you like so. The clowns had not made her laugh, unlike Brigid who found them hilarious. She'd found them almost sinister and was quite sure she'd be having nightmares over their clouds of orange hair and garish makeup for weeks to come.

Afterwards, her mam and dad had bumped into old friends they hadn't seen for a while and had stood chatting, giving the girls the opportunity to link arms and slink off toward the colourful caravans.

In hindsight, Joan could see they'd not been a good combination her and Brigid. They'd brought out a side of one another that was full of resentment at being trapped in what they saw as a little life. Both wanting more but unable to put a finger on what it was they were missing out on. They'd been eager to push boundaries and in far too much of a hurry to grow up.

Their friendship had come to an abrupt halt after that evening and Joan stared unseeingly now at the photograph as she slipped back to that fateful night at the circus.

Chapter Twenty
Joan - 1950

'It's like another world,' Joan said, jumping as the lion they'd seen prancing about doing the ringmaster's bidding grumbled at them. She watched for a moment as the big cat stalked back and forth in the tiny enclosure and felt sorry for him. She'd grumble too if she'd so little room in which to move about.

A woman in a white leotard and tights, with very red lips, leaned against a caravan smoking. She wasn't showing the slightest bit of interest in the two young girls who'd taken it upon themselves to explore an area out of bounds to the public.

'She was incredible,' Joan breathed in admiration. 'How on earth do you stand up on a horse?'

Brigid's whisper was envious. 'No idea. I wouldn't even know how to sit on one! Do you think that's a wig she's wearing? Nobody has hair that golden in real life, surely? It's a bit obvious don't you think?'

'I think she's beautiful,' Joan whispered back not sure why they were whispering because the woman was too far away to hear them.

The smell as they wound their way in deeper to where the animals were caged was strong. If she closed her eyes, Joan could imagine she was at the zoo or visiting her uncle Athol's farm.

A young man around Leonard's age was raking up the straw in one of the cages and piling it into the corner. He'd dark hair styled into a quiff and an unlit cigarette dangled from the corner of his mouth. His rolled-up shirt sleeves revealed tanned arms and Joan could see the sinewy veins standing up on his forearms as he worked.

He chose that moment to look up and his eyes, Joan thought somewhat romantically, were like glittering coals. She'd read that description in a romance novel she kept hidden under her bed. It wasn't that the book was racy it was just that she'd be embarrassed if her parents knew she read such things.

'Hello, there,' he called over in a thick accent Joan couldn't identify but thought sounded very exotic. She and Brigid had been practising their flirting lately but only on each other. There wasn't anyone worth trying out their coquettish giggles on at the youth group they both ventured down to of a Saturday night for want of something more exciting to do.

To everyone's surprise, and most of all to Joan's, she'd turned out rather attractive whereas Brigid's features had lost the childish prettiness the other girls coveted. She was more handsome than pretty these days. Mam said Joan had grown into her features, her teeth included. Joan wasn't quite sure what she was supposed to do with her blossoming looks. She felt rather like an imposter had moved in this last year and taken over the old Joan.

'Hello, yourself,' Brigid said with a flick of her hair. Her bosom seemed to grow before Joan's eyes as she sucked her tummy in for all she was worth.

Joan was determined not to be outshone and she rummaged about for something light-hearted and fun to say but all she managed to come up with was, 'The show was wonderful.'

He winked at her and she saw amusement flicker across his face.

'What was your favourite act?' he asked, leaning on the fork he'd been turning the hay over with.

'I liked the trapeze act.'

Brigid said, 'The clowns were funny.'

Joan couldn't help the shudder that passed through her at the mention of the clowns. The man, he was too old to be called a boy, noticed.

'You don't like the clowns? Everybody loves the clowns.' He grinned. His 'the' was pronounced as zee and she wondered if perhaps he was Russian. As he pretended to hook his thumbs through imaginary britches and imitated the flat-footed walk of the clowns, both girls laughed.

'So, you don't like clowns but maybe you like parties, hey?'

Neither girl had ever been to a party that didn't involve the happy birthday song and an awful wobbling blancmange. Joan spoke up, not wanting to seem childish. 'We love parties, don't we, Brigid?'

Brigid nodded that yes they did.

'This is good,' he said. 'There is a party here tonight. It is tradition the night before the circus moves on. Would you like to come?'

Joan felt a frisson of excitement at the thought of mixing with the colourful circus folk. This was it! This was what she'd been waiting for. An adventure. Something exciting, something thrilling!

The girls at school had her pegged as uptight and boring. She knew they couldn't understand why Brigid had chosen to be friends with her. She pictured the looks on their faces when they got wind of her and Brigid having been to a proper adults party and not just any party either, a wild circus after party. It thrilled her.

As quickly as the excitement had risen in her it was quashed by the voice of reason and her shoulders drooped because of course, they couldn't go. It was madness to even think about it.

Her parents would have a fit at the very idea of their daughter going to a party where there was likely to be alcohol and men past twenty. If she hadn't been so frustrated at not being able to accept the invitation, imagining the look of horror on their faces were she to ask if she could go would have made her smile.

'We'd love to come along,' Brigid replied. 'I'm Brigid and this is Joan.'

'Good, this is good. You come find me. I'll look after you. Darius. Remember that.'

'Darius,' Brigid echoed giggling. She dragged Joan off then, telling her to get the gormless look off her face.

Joan was put out. She didn't like being called gormless but she didn't understand why Brigid would say they would come when there was no way either of them would be allowed. She shot a glance at her friend, realising she knew full well she wouldn't be allowed but as for Brigid, she wasn't sure.

She'd heard her brothers ran wild. Perhaps her parents didn't keep tabs on her the way Joan's did her. She wouldn't know because she'd never met them. She didn't push for an invitation to Brigid's house any longer either, sensing her friend liked things the way they were and Joan needed Brigid far too much to upset her.

They dodged an enormous pile of manure and, looking ahead, Joan saw her parents were still engaged in conversation with their friends. 'Why did you tell him we'd come?' she demanded. 'You know we can't.'

'We could if you sneaked out.'

Joan stopped short. 'What do you mean?'

'I mean, wait for your parents to go to sleep and sneak out,' Brigid stated in a matter-of-fact manner.

Joan tried to picture herself waiting until they'd gone to bed, listening out until her dad started to snore in the rhythmic manner which meant he was asleep. Her mam was a heavy sleeper; she had to be lying next to Dad each night. Could she do it? Could she steal past their room, down the stairs and out into the night? And, and then what exactly? 'But we've no way of getting back here.'

'I could ask my brother Gerry. He's got a car and he likes a party does Gerry and I'm sure one more wouldn't be noticed.'

Joan thought of all the times she'd felt hemmed in and trapped by the boundaries her parents set around her. How sick she was of doing what was expected of her.

'We could pick you up at the bus shelter at the end of your street at eleven thirty.'

Brigid had it all figured out and Joan found herself agreeing to her plan. It would be the most daring thing she'd ever done in her life and, as they approached her parents, she hugged the thought of their secret outing to herself.

SHE'D CUT TIES WITH Brigid after that night. Ignoring her when she saw her at school and refusing to tell her why as she retreated into herself.

There were moments in one's life that defined you, Joan mused, as the photograph came back into sharp focus. That night had defined her. It had changed her forever. No matter how hard she'd tried to forget what had happened it lurked and festered. She wished with all her heart she'd never gone back to the circus.

Chapter Twenty-one
Joan, 1950

Joan lay in bed fully dressed with the sheets pulled up under her chin. Her parents seemed to be taking an age to retire this evening. She knew they weren't doing anything different. It was a night just like any other. Her guilty conscience was playing tricks on her because glancing at her bedside clock she saw it was ten twenty-five pm. They always went to bed at ten thirty on the dot and sure enough, five minutes later she heard their soft tread on the stairs along with their murmured voices as they went about their nightly routine.

She pulled the sheets a little tighter wondering if her mam might pop her head around the door to say goodnight as she did sometimes. She'd dressed in her favourite sweater, a skirt, and tights. She hoped her skirt wasn't terribly crumpled from lying down in it.

Her mam never appeared and it wasn't long before Joan heard what sounded like a train chugging down the track. Mam nodded off as soon as her head hit the pillow and how she slept through her father's trumpeting each night was beyond her, but sleep through it she did.

Tossing the covers aside, she slipped into her shoes which were at the foot of the bed then arranged the pillows into a person-shaped mound under the bedclothes. It was highly unlikely her parents would check in on her during the night but she wasn't taking any chances and, hoping it would suffice, she sat down on the edge of the bed to wait.

She'd give it a little longer to ensure they were sound asleep, Joan decided, knowing she could afford to wait given she wasn't being picked up until eleven thirty.

Her hands twisted in her lap as she sat in the darkness. Excitement mingling with trepidation swelling as she tried not to think about what would happen if she got caught. Her life wouldn't be worth living, she knew that much.

Ten minutes ticked by and, not giving herself a chance to think through what she was about to do, she stole from her room. The door closed behind her with the slightest of clicks but to Joan's paranoid ears it sounded like a thunderclap. She held her breath as she crept past her parents' bedroom pausing to listen outside the door.

There was no hiccup in the snores or creak of the bedsprings to signal one of them was getting up to see who was creeping about the place though. Not that she knew what she'd do if there was. She could have told them she was off to the toilet she supposed but how she'd explain being fully dressed when she'd gone to bed over an hour ago, she didn't know!

Down the stairs she went, managing to avoid the weak spots in the boards that would give her away. A burglar would be proud of her stealth she thought, feeling her way down the darkened hall into the kitchen where she unlatched the back door. Tilting her head, she strained her ears in the silence until she was convinced her parents hadn't woken. Then, careful not to lock the door behind her as she pulled it to, Joan stepped out into the night.

A three-quarter moon shone down on her, making her feel spotlighted as she made her way around to the side of the house where she narrowly avoided tripping over the wheelbarrow. It normally lived down the back of the garden in the shed and her heart was pounding at the thought of the clatter it would have made had she fallen over it.

When she reached the front path, she stood taking jagged breaths as she craned her neck toward her parents' window.

Her eyes burned through not blinking as she waited for a chink of light to appear beneath their curtains. None came but still, she waited, counting to one hundred before she was satisfied. Moving forward she gritted her teeth and willed the gate not to squeak as she opened it. Surely she wouldn't fall at the last hurdle?

It glided open smoothly, however, and with one final glance over her shoulder she set off down the street being careful to blend into the shadows.

The last thing she needed, having made it this far, was for an owl-like neighbour to glance out their window and catch sight of her. They'd wonder what the Walsh girl was doing out and about at such an hour and feel obliged to check in with her parents.

It was with relief she reached the bus stop with no shouted cry from an opened window having sounded. She sat down and jiggled her legs which were twitching with anticipation. She wished she smoked, anything to steady her nerves.

The minutes felt like hours and Joan had decided that Brigid must have changed her mind or had been unable to talk her brother into driving them back to Terenure. She'd gotten up to go, unsure whether she was relieved or disappointed when she heard a car's engine break the stillness. She was caught in the headlights that swung into the street and fear washed over her.

What if it was a neighbour coming home from a late-night soiree? How would she explain herself? The car slowed and did a U-turn pulling in alongside where she waited. Seeing Brigid's excited face in the passenger window she clambered in the back.

'You made it.' Brigid twisted in her seat. 'I wasn't sure if you would.'

'I said I would.' Joan was short, she didn't want to appear babyish to Brigid's brother.

'This is my brother Gerry. Gerry, this is Joan.'

'Howya?' Gerry asked, not sounding overly interested as he glanced back at her before turning away to blow a plume of smoke out the window. Even though Joan couldn't make out his features too well in the darkened car interior, she could see he'd the same nose as Brigid. It wouldn't look at all well on a boy she thought, settling back in her seat as Brigid chattered on non-stop.

Her friend was nervous for all her bravado, Joan realised. It was then her body went goosy and her scalp prickled. She'd a bad feeling and the words, 'I don't think this was such a good idea after all' formed but she didn't let them spill forth. She was being silly. She wasn't superstitious. Sure, it was an adventure, she told herself. They'd be grand.

Only she wasn't.

Chapter Twenty-two

Joan, 1950

Gerry bumped the car along to a section of the field that had been reserved for circus goers to park earlier. Now it was deserted. He stilled the engine and the girls climbed out to stand beside the car.

Joan eyed Gerry. He'd a sly look about him she decided, as Brigid nudged her and pointed.

In the distance they could see a bonfire, it was a beacon to where the faint shouts and laughter of partygoers sounded. It was a good job there were no neighbours in the immediate vicinity or the gardai would have long since swung by to tell them to quieten down, Joan thought.

Gerry locked the car and the trio picked their way across the field, moths to the flame.

A record player was set up outside one of the caravans and a couple in all their finery performed fancy footwork to the big band music playing while a small group clapped them on. Joan felt very young watching them.

Moving on, she eyed the remains of a spread that had long since been swooped on and wished she'd eaten her own dinner. She'd been far too anxious for meat and potatoes though and she'd feigned being full from the treats she'd wolfed at the circus. Her mam had let her off.

The flames of the bonfire flickered and spat as someone tossed wood on it and they stood on the fringe of the laughing, chattering crowd, illuminated by the fireside glow.

Darius spied them and called out. Seeing his handsome face grinning in welcome, Joan's earlier fears melted away as he ushered them to squeeze in alongside him.

Darius bantered away to Joan, putting her at ease. This was exactly where she belonged she decided, feeling wild and free-spirited as she accepted the hip flask he passed her way.

She'd never tasted spirits before, and she didn't much like the way whatever was in the flask burned her throat and made her eyes water, but she managed not to cough as did Brigid and their initial sips soon turned into swigs as they whispered together that it didn't taste all that bad.

They'd giggled over what the girls at school would have to say when they relayed their adventure over the weekend come Monday.

Brigid was sitting on her right talking to a lad called Stefan who fancied himself far too much in Joan's opinion. His English was heavily accented like Darius's as he talked up his role as maintenance man for the circus. She supposed it was important. She wouldn't want to be swinging off a dodgy trapeze, and Brigid clearly thought so. She was hanging off his every word.

He and Stefan were both from Romania she learned hyperaware of Darius's shoulder brushing against hers each time he handed her the flask. Somebody in the huddle launched into a song in a language Joan didn't recognise but she clapped along with everybody else, swept up in the joviality.

Gerry was no longer sitting with them she saw, beginning to feel a little woozy and unsure of how long they'd been sitting by the fire. She swung her gaze around and thought she saw him standing with a group passing a cigarette around near one of the caravans but the haze from the bonfire made her uncertain.

The general gaiety of the party was interspersed with blood-curdling shrieks which at first had startled her but Darius had reassured her it was just the monkeys making their presence known.

She was enjoying the dreamlike feeling beginning to steal over her. She'd a smile on her face and was full of love for everyone. Brigid nudged her and said she and Stefan were going to see if they could bum a couple of cigarettes and she thought it very funny given Brigid didn't smoke. She watched them go, aware that Darius had moved closer, dropping his arm around her shoulder.

Someone was dancing like a whirling dervish and watching the spinning woman she began to feel queasy. The flames danced higher, licking and splitting into two as if taunting her, and the faces smattered around the fire were cloning one another before merging back into one again. She was overheating and she fanned her hand in front of her face before blinking hard. She was filled with the urge to move away from the group for some fresh air. That would make her feel better.

So, when Darius suggested they go for a walk, she let him help her up, grateful for his steadying arm as she staggered. He led her away from the hubbub until they were on the edge of the cluster of caravans, all in darkness.

Joan swallowed as saliva filled beneath her tongue and she prayed she wasn't going to make a fool of herself by being sick. She gulped at the cool night air and it helped marginally.

'I think you've had too much to drink.' Darius laughed as Joan nodded.

'You poor girl.' He pulled her to him and kissed her. Joan responded. His lips were soft but as his mouth pressed hard over hers and his tongue prised her lips open she tasted stale cigarettes and booze. She felt the bile rising in her belly and pushed at him, feeling panicked. He gripped her harder.

She managed to wrench her head back, 'No, Darius. I'd like to go back to the others now.' She swung her head around so his mouth landed on her hair and he growled something she didn't understand. She tried to wriggle free of his grasp but it was vice-like and she was pushed down on the ground, aware of a sharp stone digging into her back. Her skirt was rucked up and rough hands grabbed at her.

Joan tried to wriggle free but he was much stronger than her. This must be happening to someone else she thought, opening her mouth to cry out, but her scream was muted by his hand clamping down over her mouth.

She stared up at the inky sky throughout the assault and when it was over she lay there, ignoring the hand he offered to help her up. He shrugged and walked off. She didn't move until she was sure he was gone and then rolling to her side she vomited until her stomach ached with emptiness.

She forced herself to stand, aching and bruised, as she tried to tidy herself before limping back to the party to find Brigid.

Brigid had had enough of Stefan who was flirting with the woman with the golden hair and a talent for riding bareback.

Despite her inebriated state she registered something was wrong when she saw Joan and she rallied up Gerry who reluctantly dragged himself away to drive them home.

Brigid sat quietly in the front seat as the alcohol she'd consumed caught up with her. Gerry growled at her not to be sick in his car while Joan sat stoically in the back seat. Empty.

She stared out the window, vowing not to cry, because to do so would be to admit to what had happened.

She'd decided, as she tiptoed back into the house and locked herself in the bathroom to wash herself, that this evening had never happened. She would put it from her mind.

JOAN STUFFED THE PHOTOGRAPHS back into the envelope she'd found them in. Yes, she thought, sliding the envelope out of sight down the inside of the box where she'd found it, there were moments in life that defined you.

She'd make her excuses to Gordon, she decided. She'd drop a note in his letterbox to apologise for having forgotten she was otherwise engaged. How could she accept? To do so would mean she would be expected to return his invitation and she couldn't possibly do that. If he knew her secrets, he'd have never suggested tea in the first place.

Chapter Twenty-three

Moira had slept in this morning, partly because it was Sunday and she always slept in on a Sunday; it was sacrilege not to in her opinion, and partly because there'd been nothing much to get up for. She awoke to the sound of rain battering the windows and the wind moaning, and snuggled back down under the covers. *Bliss.*

The Indian summer had broken, she thought, which was all the excuse she needed to snooze away another hour or so. Then, the realisation Tom was not next to her hit her afresh and she reached groggily for her phone. There were no missed calls and, frustrated, she tossed it down the end of the bed. Hurt bubbled deep inside her.

Tom wasn't stubborn by nature but she was and as such it was up to him to come to her and explain his behaviour. She placed her hands on her tummy. It still didn't feel real. She supposed it wouldn't until she started to get big and the baby began to do somersaults or whatever it was babies got up to in there.

She tried to divert her thoughts. What was it Rosi always said to remember when your, thoughts were running away on yer? It was something about them not defining you. They were just passing through. Everything would be okay. 'Everything will be okay,' she whispered.

The curious sight she'd witnessed late yesterday afternoon sprang to mind. She'd ventured out of her room after Mammy and Donal left, unable to stop herself from going to the window to see whether Tom happened to be making his way down the street with an enormous bouquet of 'I'm sorry I behaved like an eejit' flowers. There was no sign of him but there'd been a horde of people milling about on the pavement below.

It was then her mouth had dropped open as she'd registered Mammy was down there gesticulating like she was giving a sermon. She'd been tempted to go downstairs and see what was happening for herself but she'd had enough of everyone and had dragged her feet toward the kitchen in search of sustenance.

Her brain was like a sieve at the moment too because she'd planned to ring Mammy last night but after she'd eaten she'd gone to bed and slept soundly despite the turmoil of the afternoon. She'd have to telephone her this morning and see what it was all about.

Maybe Mammy would let her move in with her and Donal. Then, as she thought about the possibility of hearing their headboard banging she vetoed the idea before it could grow legs. Aisling would get over herself. She'd have to.

Her reaction yesterday had been childish. It wasn't as if Moira had gotten herself in the family way on purpose, she'd not done it to spite her sister and besides, it wasn't a fecking competition. She mentally stuffed her sister in the same arse basket in which Tom was currently placed.

She heard the front door close and knew the routines of the household well enough to guess Quinn had just returned with the Sunday papers he liked to pore over.

Hearing a shriek a beat later, she jumped. What was that all about? Her ears burned, trying to hear what was going on. Could it have been a mouse? Aisling was a shrieker when it came to vermin, *hmm and other things*.

Muffled voices sounded but she couldn't make out what was going on and she was damned if she was going to get up and be on the receiving end of that awful duck's arse face Aisling pulled when she was in a mood.

Ten minutes or so passed before she heard the front door go, followed by a silence which Moira hoped meant Aisling and Quinn had ventured downstairs. Either way, she had to get up because she needed the loo.

The apartment was satisfyingly empty and Moira set about making a cup of tea, dropping two slices of bread into the toaster having forgotten all about the cry she'd heard earlier. As she waited for the kettle to boil she spied the papers on the table, unopened.

Strange. Quinn usually took them downstairs to read in the dining room. He and Aisling liked to linger over one of Mrs Baicu's cooked breakfasts on a Sunday. He'd leave behind the Who's Who and Who was Seen doing What, Where sections for Moira. He could be thoughtful even if he did leave the toilet seat up.

Tightening the belt on her dressing gown she padded over to have a look through, finding herself frozen statue-like as the front-page headline slapped her eyeballs.

'Christ on a bike,' she muttered, blinking rapidly in case hallucinating was a symptom of early pregnancy. No, it would appear not because the words glaring up at her still read:

'Guesthouse Owner Denies Knowledge of Hollywood A-Lister Affair Under her Roof'

Beneath the bold black type was a black and white image of Mammy. She'd sucked her cheeks in the way Aisling did when she'd been trying to give herself cheekbones and was doing something in between the splits and a lunge. It was as though the people gathered about had been chanting the limbo song, 'How low can you go?' and Mammy was showing off like she always did when challenged.

She hastily skimmed over the article in which Maureen denied having any Hollywood celebrities staying at O'Mara's which, she added was a reputable establishment. The rest of the story was speculation as to an affair between Jenny Seymour and Jackson Creed who were in Dublin to promote their latest film. Jackson's wife, at home in Los Angeles, had issued a 'no comment' statement.

Moira tore her gaze away from the newspaper as understanding of what had had her sister shrieking earlier sank in. She picked up the phone which was lying discarded on the table which Moira took to mean Aisling had already given out to Mammy and she hit redial.

Maureen's wary voice answered after a few rings.

'Mammy, it's me, Moira.'

'I know who it is, Moira. What do you want?'

'I'm mortified, so I am! I'll have you know your future grandchild won't be able to show his or her face at the nursery school. Not with a nana making a holy show of herself doing the gymnastics on the front page of the papers. What did you think you were doing?'

Maureen sighed and held the phone away from her ear which was still red from the bashing Aisling had given it not ten minutes earlier. 'What does it look like I was doing?'

'I told you, gymnastics for senior cits.'

Aisling had said she'd looked like she was trying to be the poster girl for knee replacements given the depth of the lunge she'd achieved.

It was a blessing Donal had been on hand to help her back up because in her excitement she'd put her all into her lunge seeing not only her modelling debut but a prime Mo-pant marketing opportunity and as such she'd nearly done the splits. It was not good at her time of life.

Mercifully, by the time she'd realised she was stuck and had flapped her hand for Donal to rescue her, the cameras had stopped clicking. The paps as she was now calling them had realised she wasn't the hot Hollywood superstar in the throes of a torrid affair with a fellow hot Hollywood superstar as per the tip-off they'd received but rather a little Irish woman wearing yoga pants and doing strange dance moves.

She relived her moment of glory.

'Who are you?' A long-haired, scruffy man with bad teeth had demanded, pen poised over pad.

'I'm not sure I like your tone.' Maureen had fixed him with a steely gaze.

'Erm, who are you, *please*?'

'That's more like it. I'm Maureen O'Mara.' She'd tossed this back importantly wishing Donal would hurry up and help her right herself. It was hard to be authoritative when you were stuck like so.

Their minds were in tune with one another she thought as a split second later he stepped out of the shadows and eased her upright.

'Is this your guesthouse?' yer scruffy wan demanded forgetting his manners once again.

Maureen jiggled her legs in an effort to ease the cramp. 'In a round-about way. My daughter Aisling manages O'Mara's for me these days; it's been in the family for generations but she's in a sulk in her bedroom at the moment.'

An excited cry from a younger male reporter went up, 'I don't believe it! Demi Moore's up there, look!' He was craning his neck back, his finger pointing skywards. Another flurry of clicking sounded.

Maureen took a few steps forward so as she could see what had them all in a blather. She angled her head to stare up at the window. 'No, no, that's not Demi, that's Moira. My youngest daughter. She's got herself into a little bit of hot water which is why her sister's in a sulk but sure, they'll both be grand.' Maureen realised as the attention once more settled on her that she had a prime opportunity here with Ireland's media at her feet.

She took a moment to compose herself, arranging her face into an earnest, heartbroken mammy expression and with pleading eyes urged yer bad teeth one, 'Take this down, son. Tom, if you're listening, it's not too late to sort things out with Moira. I know she can be a moody mare but she needs you as does your little one. You need to come and see her. You've some talking to do the pair of you.'

There was a whispering amongst the crowd but nobody asked, who's Tom? and annoyingly yer long-haired fella didn't take notes.

'Is Jenny Seymour staying at O'Mara's?' a woman called out.

They were a rude lot these reporters, Maureen thought, miffed. She wasn't one to fib but while she was happy to divulge the ins and outs of her family's dramas she'd fight tooth and nail to protect her guests' privacy.

'Not at all. What are youse on about? And you can clear off now. Cluttering up the pavements you are. I'll get the council on to you, so I will.'

'Mammy!'

Maureen came back to the present as she realised Moira was still bleating at her.

'What?'

'I don't get it though. Why would they think Jenny Seymour was doing the riding with Jackson Creed here at O'Mara's?'

Maureen rolled her eyes and scratched behind Pooh's ears. Moira could be very slow on the uptake at times. 'Because Jenny Seymour checked in to room ten under a false name and yer man Jackson called in to see her.'

'So, they are having a fling?'

'How would I know? You'll have to ask your sister that.'

Moira pursed her lips. That would be tricky given she wasn't talking to her.

Chapter Twenty-four

Maureen had been burning up the phone line to Roisin in the week that had passed since the failed family conference and the love-triangle scandal had broken in the tabloids.

It had all come out in the end as these things do, she'd tutted to Donal, holding up the newspaper full of the breaking news that Hollywood's sweetheart was a homewrecker.

Jenny Seymour had been whisked away on a private jet back to Hollywood as had Jack Kennedy (Donal had corrected her on this point. 'It's Jackson *Creed*, Mo.' She'd ignored him).

Maureen felt Jenny Seymour was getting the raw end of the deal and she'd said, 'It takes two to tango,' to Roisin that morning. She'd rung her with an update on her annus horribilis week.

Tom and Moira had yet to contact one another. Aisling and Moira still weren't speaking despite her having words with them both. Quinn had been on the phone too, asking her what she thought he should do as he was fed up with the frosty atmosphere in the apartment, but failing banging both their heads together, she was at a loss, she'd informed Roisin in between bites of her morning toast.

Roisin had stopped listening at a certain two words. 'Mammy, don't be saying things like annus horribilis. It's horrible.'

Maureen had been indignant, spluttering toast crumbs as she said, 'Listen to me, Rosi, if it's good enough for the queen to bandy about when the going gets tough, it's good enough for me.' And, she'd added, 'Was it her fault she'd a daughter whose mind resided in the gutter? Sure, everybody knew the French had different words for things, annus had nothing to do with your bottom.'

'It's Latin, Mammy,' Roisin had replied.

'Don't be clever with me, Roisin,' Maureen bounced back.

Unfortunately for them both, Noah, who'd been poking lettuce leaves into Mr Nibbles, his gerbil's cage at the time this conversation was taking place had seized on what was clearly an inappropriate word. He'd rolled it around in his head liking the sound of it and had even whispered it to Mr Nibbles, receiving what he liked to think was a two-toothed grin from the gerbil as he paused in his gnawing of the lettuce. Then he'd stored it away waiting for the right moment in which to drop it.

It came that very afternoon, which was why Roisin was bellowing down the phone to her mammy now, eight hours after their earlier conversation.

'Mammy, I'm just after dropping Noah off at his Granny Quealey's and do you know what he said to her?'

Maureen had had a busy day. She'd been perusing homeware stores with Donal because they'd decided their new home would suit a Cape Cod look. Donal had mentioned he was worried she had a bit of a Kennedy fixation because sure, everybody knew they'd had a beach house on the Cape. Maureen had assured him it was nothing to do with the Kennedys and that she was partial to the nautical style was all. As such, new furniture was required.

Now she rotated her ankles, which were protesting at having been traipsed about the shops, as she sat on the sofa nursing a cup of coffee Donal had made her.

She was trying to ignore Pooh who kept glancing balefully at her and then the front door, his lead clenched between his teeth. It was his own fault, she thought. If he was nicer to Donal, he'd gladly take him for a walk but the last time he'd volunteered, Pooh had cocked his leg and done his business on Donal's new loafers.

Donal said he swore if Pooh could talk he'd have said, 'Take that interloper.'. It was written all over his sly, poodly face, Donal had said.

Maureen had been very annoyed because it had taken her an age to convince Donal that loafers were a good look on him, on any man for that matter. She'd told him yer Dustin Hoffman wan had made loafers acceptable footwear for men in the seventies.

They'd come close to having words over that because Donal brought up that Dustin Hoffman had also starred in a certain movie called *Tootsie* where he'd gotten around dressed as a woman which didn't say much for the loafer.

The loafers were a moot point now, they'd had to go in the bin.

'Mammy, are you listening to me?'

Maureen didn't like the edge she was detecting in her eldest daughter's voice. 'Of course I am but it was a silly question, wasn't it. How can I know what Noah said to his granny when I wasn't there at the time, Roisin?'

'It was a figure of speech, Mammy.' Roisin sighed heavily and got to the point of her call. 'He said, and I quote, 'I've had a horrible anus week, Granny, thank you for asking.' Then, she took me aside and asked if he was suffering the worms and that I needed to get him to stop playing with that gerbil and chewing on his nails.'

Maureen bit down on her lip, imagining the horrified expression on her daughter's dour ex-mammy-in-law's face. She couldn't help herself and she called out to Donal. 'Donal, listen to this you'll never believe what Noah's after saying to his sourpuss granny over there in London.'

Roisin heard Donal's rumbling laugh as Maureen repeated her grandson's words. The sound of his laughter usually made her smile because he had the sort of belly laugh that reminded her of Father Christmas. Right now though, she was in no mood for humour.

'Don't be saying the annus horribilis again, Mammy, alright?'

There was no answer.

'Mammy!'

'Alright, alright. Now then, what are we going to do about your sisters?'

OVER AT O'MARA'S, QUINN was getting thoroughly fed up with the prickly atmosphere when either his wife or sister-in-law were in the room at the same time. He'd tried his best to jolly them along but they were both stubborn and refused to break the tension. He'd even had a quiet word with his mammy-in-law who had given him the sage advice to bang their heads together to make the pair of them see sense. He hadn't taken her advice.

Maureen had given them what for down the telephone but it had no effect and the last he'd heard, Roisin was threatening to come over and sort them out.

All this being out of sorts with one another had had a knock-on effect too whereby Aisling, in her current frame of mind, was no longer interested in the riding.

It was feast or famine with her, he sighed, glancing at his watch. He'd be off to the restaurant in a moment.

Aisling was dunking a biscuit in her tea and he watched as the soggy end broke off and fell into her cup. She did that funny thing she did with her mouth when she was annoyed. It reminded him of a duck's arse and put him in no mood for the riding either. He'd come home for the couple of hours between the lunch and dinner rush to try to talk her round and perhaps go for a quick gallop around the track but neither was on the cards.

Quinn sighed and drained his cuppa before getting up from the table and dropping a kiss on top of his wife's head. 'Time for me to go, Ash.' He paused, breathing in the apple smell of her shampoo. She didn't answer, too busy trying to retrieve the bits of biscuit floating in the bottom of her cup with her teaspoon.

Quinn made for the door, turning before he reached the hall. 'She's not done it to spite you, Ash, you know that, right?'

Aisling put her teaspoon down and looked at her husband. 'I know.'

'Then why are you freezing her out. It was an accident and she's scared stiff. You know what Moira's like. She covers it up by being bolshie. She needs you.'

He'd a point, Aisling thought, feeling a tug of guilt at the way she'd behaved. It wasn't like her but she'd not been able to help herself.

Her bottom lip quivered ominously and Quinn quickly added, 'You'll feel better if you patch things up with her.' He made a hasty exit in case she started to cry properly. He'd a restaurant to run and he couldn't very well stay home mopping up tears over something only Aisling could put right.

Aisling listened to the door close behind him. She'd felt like her insides had had origami performed on them this past week as she'd tried to process Moira's shock news. She'd behaved appallingly, she knew she had, but she was an O'Mara and the O'Mara women hated having to back down.

Dear Aisling,

I'm envious of the fact my sister is pregnant and I'm not. Does this make me an awful, bitter person? The thing is when she told the family the news, I felt like a knife was twisting in my stomach and I didn't say a word. I walked away from her and now I don't know how to come back from that. What should I do?'

Yours faithfully,

Me

Aisling sighed because no answer was forthcoming.

Chapter Twenty-five

Moira was on the telephone to Andrea. She'd a jar of peanut butter and half a loaf of bread on her bedside table for sustenance and she'd been working her way through it, in between bending Andrea's ear about her own annus horribilis week.

She was sitting propped up with pillows on her bed. She'd the curtains open even though it was nearly dark. With a glance around her room, she scowled. She was getting fed up with staring at the same four walls but she wasn't game to venture out and be on the receiving end of Aisling's cold shoulder again either.

Last night she'd decided she'd as much right to the sofa as her sister and so they'd sat in silence through *Fair City*, all the things unsaid between them hanging heavy on the air. As the show's credits came rolling down the screen, Moira realised she'd sat staring at the screen but she couldn't tell you a thing that had just happened on her favourite soap. It was hopeless. She'd had to ring Mammy and get her to relay the crucial parts which had also meant listening to a lecture about how friends could come and go but a sister was for life. She'd told Mammy she didn't deserve a life sentence and as such, she'd like the parole, thank you very much.

She was loath to admit it but Aisling freezing her out hurt. It hurt as much as the wound Tom had inflicted by not reaching out to her. In fact, it hurt more, because while she'd thought she could count on Tom she'd *known* her sisters would have her back. It was always them against Mammy and the world but not this time.

Roisin was trying to be neutral which was very annoying because she should be on Moira's side. She told this to Andrea. 'She's not fecking Switzerland, she's my big sister and as such, she should take my side.'

'Ah, it can't be easy for her being in the middle of you and Aisling like.'

'Sometimes you have to stop playing piggy in the middle and take a side. My side. The world does not revolve around Aisling O'Mara,' Moira mumbled through her mouthful of sandwich. She was being unfair because Roisin refused to be drawn on the subject of her middle sister behaving like an arse but she was proving to be very enthusiastic about Noah having a cousin on the way. It was nice.

'She's been ringing me every day and I know it's because she cares but she brings up the birth side of having a baby all the time and to be honest, Andrea, I'd rather not think about it. I mean what if my baby gets the O'Mara pumpkin-head gene. I'll be ruined down yonder.'

'Ah, Moira, I'm sure your baby will have a head the size of a pea and just pop on out. Besides, it's a natural part of life; your bits won't be ruined. They'll be good as new after a week or so.'

'I hope so. Rosi's after demonstrating all this breathing for when I'm in labour because she says it helps but I think she's getting ahead of herself. There's plenty of time for that. She puffs and pants down the line and it's like getting an obscene, heavy breathing call each night from your sister.'

Andrea laughed. 'Will you go to the classes like?'

'The heavy breathing ones?'

'Yes, the ones that get you ready for it all.'

'I don't know. What if Tom and I don't sort something out? Don't people normally go in couples to those? I don't want to be the sad one on her beanbag who has to partner with the teacher.'

'I'll be your plus one,' Andrea stated loyally.

Moira tried to say thank you but the masticated sandwich was stuck to the roof of her mouth and the words came out garbled.

'Are you having another peanut butter sandwich?'

Moira frantically worked at the blob of bread managing to dislodge it. 'Yes, I'm eating for two remember? Do you know, it's strange but I was never all that partial to peanut butter sandwiches but now I can't stop eating them. Do you think that's my first proper craving?'

'I don't know but I do know you'll get constipated if you keep that up. My mam always says peanuts bind you up.'

Moira carried on eating. She was regular as clockwork, peanuts or no peanuts. She was stretched out on her bed and was beginning to feel like a prisoner in her bedroom. *Bally K* was on soon but she didn't fancy a repeat of last night's sitting in Siberia.

'Has the other business settled down?'

'What business?'

'The,' Andrea lowered her voice to a whisper, 'sex scandal at an Irish guesthouse.' She quoted the particularly lurid headline one of the more salacious tabloids had run with.

'I don't know what the big deal was. Nobody in Hollywood can keep it in their trousers, everybody knows that,' Moira snorted. She changed the subject. 'I didn't tell you, did I? Mammy and Donal are after finding a house. Mammy says it has a proper sea view and she's very excited about it all. She says it's a Cape Codder whatever that is.'

'Da, dah, de, dah, dah, dah, dah,' Andrea hummed the wedding march tune.

'Ah, don't be doing that, not with me in my delicate condition.'

'Sorry.'

'And don't be giving out about Mammy living her best life either.'

'I won't. Is it child friendly?'

'I don't know, why?'

'Because, you eejit, you're going to be needing your mammy to babysit.'

It was a good point. 'I'll have to check. They don't take possession until after Christmas so if it's not, I've plenty of time to talk them into something suitable for a baby.'

'What are you going to do about Aisling? One of you will have to be the first to wave the white flag.'

Moira didn't say anything.

'C'mon, Moira, you can see where she's coming from.'

'No, I can't, she's being a selfish mare. It's me who needs the tender loving care. And you're supposed to be *my* friend.'

'I am your friend which is why I'm after getting to you make things up with her. Think about it for a minute. She's desperate for a baby and you're not even thinking about it and boom it happens for you.'

Moira frowned. She could see where Andrea was coming from but still—she decided to change the subject.

'Have you seen Connor Reid since the, you know?'

'Since we were nearly arrested for shoplifting a pregnancy testing kit?'

Moira cringed. 'We'll laugh about it one day.'

'I won't. And yes. It's been awful. He gives me this look that's half sympathetic and half shock every time I see him. It was the talk of the office which means he told mealy-mouthed Melva and she told all the other secretaries. I felt like I had a scarlet letter branded on my forehead.'

'Well, you've risen above all the tittle-tattle, good for you.' Moira sounded like Mammy and she knew it.

'No, I haven't. If anyone asked I told them the kit was for you.'

'Andrea!'

'What? It's not you who has to show your face there every day. I broke when Nora asked if I wanted to talk. She was trying to be understanding but it was very, very creepy.'

Moira tried to imagine the taxation solicitor being understanding and knew if she'd been in Andrea's shoes she'd have snapped too.

Moira squirmed; she needed the loo, she'd have to go. 'Listen, I've got to go, Andrea, I've turned into a right Woolworths bladder these last few days.'

'Okay, but promise me you'll patch things up with Aisling. You'll feel better if you do, Moira. And I hope you hear from Tom.'

'I've got to go,' Moira said, disconnecting the call and rolling off the bed to visit the bathroom.

She was washing her hands when she risked a glance in the mirror. She looked pasty and tired. She was tired. Tired and sad.

Chapter Twenty-six

Moira did miss Aisling. She desperately wanted to pour her heart out as to how much it hurt her that Tom was ignoring her. She'd been brave and telephoned him when she got in from college, knowing he'd be home studying or, at least he usually would've been. She knew his routines. There'd been no answer though.

It had been so very anticlimactic. She'd spent an age psyching herself up into making the call, rehearsing what she'd say, only for him not to pick up. She wondered if he was otherwise engaged or whether he'd seen it was her and decided not to answer.

College had been a struggle today too. She'd hardly been able to keep her eyes open. She hadn't expected to feel as tired as she was but at least she wasn't throwing up. She'd not felt in the teeniest bit sick so that was something.

Mammy was on at her to make an appointment with her GP to make sure she was fit and well but at the moment the thought of having to make a trip to the doctors just seemed too hard. Everything was too hard.

What she wanted with all her heart right at this moment was to flop down next to Ash on the sofa and for her sister to open a bag of Snowballs for them to share. It was the only thing that would make her feel better.

She'd gone straight to her room when she'd gotten in that afternoon and, kicking her shoes off, had flopped down on her bed. She'd mulled over all the things she wanted to say to Tom, whispering them out loud into the silent bedroom and after the disappointment of not hearing his voice, she'd closed her eyes.

Fatigue had washed over her and she must have drifted off because the sounds outside the room were different now and she could smell garlic. Her stomach growled. That was another thing, she was always hungry. The rate she was shovelling food in her gob she'd be the size of a bus by the time she got to March.

She lay there for a minute and thought about what Andrea had said to her. It didn't seem as if Aisling was going to knock on her door and instigate a reconciliation and she'd had enough, she realised. She wanted her sister to talk to. She needed her sister, and as such, it would seem she was going to have to be the one to swallow her pride.

Moira got up and stretched, wondering how it was possible to have had a nap and feel even more tired than she had before. She moved over to her drawers and, opening the top one, rummaged around until she found what she was after.

Without giving herself time to change her mind she flung open her door and strode forth waving a pair of white knickers. She wished she'd a pair of Mammy's bloomers to hand. They'd have made a much better flag!

Aisling was chasing onions and garlic around the frying pan when Moira ventured into the living room. Catching movement out the corner of her eye she looked up from what she was doing and saw her sister looking pale and drawn, flapping a white G-string about the place. She stared at her wondering what on earth she was up to.

'Why are you waving a G-string at me?'

Moira was jubilant, Aisling had spoken to her! 'It's my white flag, I would've liked to borrow a pair of Mammy's knickers, they'd have made a much better flag.' Moira shrugged.

'Sail more like,' Aisling muttered.

Humour was definitely a sign her sister was thawing and Moira decided to roll with it blurting out, 'If you stop behaving like an arse then I will too. Peace?'

Moira looked very young and uncertain, Aisling thought, giving her the once over. She was also pale and there was no glimpse of her usual sparkle. Then, realising she was expected to reply, she said, 'But I haven't said anything in the least bit arsey.' She couldn't help the sanctimonious expression she knew had settled on her face because it was true. She returned to her frying.

She hadn't said anything at all and they'd not had words because Aisling hadn't known what to say to her sister. The sense of unfairness at the situation had agitated with each passing day and she'd not trusted herself to speak.

'*Exactly*. You've been giving me the silent treatment and that's worse than if you'd yelled at me and got what you wanted to say off your chest.'

Aisling turned and pulled a face but didn't say anything. She knew Moira was right. She'd behaved like a spoiled child who'd not gotten her own way but Moira could be insensitive to those around her too. She'd never been good at reading other people's emotions.

'And don't be giving me the duck's arse face either. I hate that too.'

'I don't look like a duck's arse.'

'You do when you do that thing with your mouth.'

'I don't do anything with my mouth.'

'Yes, you do. You do this.' Moira arranged her mouth so her upper lip curled like Aisling's just had and she stared hard at her sister.

Aisling frowned. 'That's nothing like a duck's arse. I don't know where you got that from that's yer man Billy Idol doing his Rebel Yell face.'

Moira's face broke into a grin at that. 'Do you remember when Pat thought he looked like yer man Billy when he bleached his hair and got about in those leather trousers and that ripped singlet even though it was fecking freezing?'

Aisling's mouth twitched at the memory. 'Mammy was always threatening to cut them off him. You were only young then, I'm surprised you remember.'

'How could I not remember my brother fist punching the air and scowling as he pranced about in those smelly things. Disgusting they were.' Moira shuddered. 'And they squeaked when he walked.'

'I remember. I was never sure whether he'd let off or if it was the trousers,' Aisling said, shaking her head as she added, 'He drove Mammy mad doing the air-punching and that face. She'd say she'd give him her own rebel yell, one he'd never forget if he didn't cut it out.'

Moira hummed the tune to Rebel Yell and Aisling, unable to help herself, made a fist and did the air-punching thing as she sang the more, more, more chorus. 'What an eejit he was,' Aisling said when she'd finished.

Moira loved her brother dearly but she had to concur. 'Aisling, I'm sorry.' She was as surprised as Aisling at the words that had popped from her mouth. It was so out of character.

Aisling looked at her sister then. Her sister who never said sorry. She caught the lost look in her eyes and a surge of shame rose up over the way she'd been treating her. Her, a grown woman. She didn't deserve to be responsible for another human being carrying on like so. 'You've nothing to be sorry for, Moira. I've been a horrible sister.'

'Yes, you have.' Moira moved them back onto familiar territory. 'In fact, Ash, you've been an annus horribilis sister.'

Roisin had told them both on separate calls about Mammy's favourite new catchphrase and Noah's delight in flinging it about in front of his granny.

The two sisters eyed one another and for a moment neither was sure whether they were going to laugh or cry. They went with the first and were clutching their sides, bent double, with Aisling screeching she was going to wet her knickers by the time Moira pointed to the pan which was beginning to smoke ominously on the stove.

'Jaysus,' Aisling cried, rushing knock kneed over to turn the element off.

Dinner was abandoned in favour of peanut butter sandwiches and Moira watched delightedly once they'd polished off several rounds of bread as Aisling hauled herself off the sofa. She went into the kitchen and told her not to look because she was after getting something down from her secret hiding place.

Moira did as she was told. She'd no need to peek because she already knew where Aisling's secret Snowball stash was hidden.

Aisling returned with an unopened bag and she settled herself back down on the sofa next to her sister. She ripped the seal off and held the packet so as Moira could delve in. She took two and with one stuffed inside either cheek, said, 'I'm sorry I made you feel like I was stealing your thunder, Ash. I should have been more sensitive to your situation but you know it was Mammy's idea to hold a stupid family conference in the first place. I'd barely had time for it to sink in myself and then there was the way Tom reacted.'

Aisling smiled to herself as she too snaffled a Snowball. This was the Moira she knew and loved. The one always eager to pass the buck.

'And, Ash, I didn't get pregnant on purpose. Believe me, I didn't. I have no idea how it happened.'

Aisling raised an eyebrow.

'Okay, I mean I know how it happened but it wasn't supposed to happen. It feels like it's happening to someone else.' Moira chewed frantically before helping herself again. The chocolate was hitting her system and it was comforting but the weight of the mess she was in was sitting heavily on her.

'I can't believe Tom doesn't want to know about it. I didn't expect him to jump for joy when I told him. I mean, like I said, it wasn't planned but I thought we were solid. I thought we'd work it out and it'd all be okay.'

Aisling knew how it felt when the person you loved turned out to be a stranger. She'd been engaged to Marcus before she and Quinn had gotten together but had been let down badly. It was a blessing she knew now but it hadn't felt like it at the time. She shook the bag at Moira.

Moira hadn't finished what was in her mouth but she took another two, nonetheless.

'I can't be a mammy all on my own.'

'You won't be on your own, Moira, you know that. You've got all of us.'

'But I want Tom,' she wailed. 'I love him, Ash. What am I going to do?'

Aisling pulled her sister to her and let her sob it out, making soothing noises, and when Moira's tears had ebbed away to sniffs she asked, 'What did he say when you gave him the news.'

Moira got up and retrieved the tissues from the top of the fridge and gave her nose a good blow before coming to sit back down. She relayed their conversation and filled her sister in on her attempt to call him this evening. 'I think he was there. He just didn't want to talk to me.'

'He hasn't been in work this week either, Quinn told me.'

Moira looked at her sister through red-rimmed eyes. That was so out of character for Tom. Mr Reliable. How could she have got him so wrong?

'And you haven't spoken to him since you told him?'

Moira shook her head mournfully.

The phone rang then and Moira shot up to answer it. Maybe Tom had seen he'd missed her call and was ringing her back.

'Hello?' she answered with a hiccup.

'Moira, it's me, Roisin. The malt vinegar is very good for the hiccups. Let's run through the breathing for riding out the contractions.'

'Rosi, feck off *Bally K* is about to start.'

QUINN CLAMBERED INTO bed next to Aisling who hadn't been asleep. She snuggled up next to him. 'I made it up with Moira.'

He gave her a squeeze, 'Thank God for that. Do you know if she's sorted things out with Tom?'

'No, she tried to phone him earlier but he didn't answer.'

Quinn sighed and Aisling felt his breath tickle the top of her head.

'What is it?'

'I told you he hadn't been in work all week?'

'Yeah.' Aisling was wide awake now.

'Well, he's after handing his notice in.'

'Poor Moira. He really is avoiding her. I've a good mind to go around to his house and give him a piece of my mind.'

Chapter Twenty-seven

Bronagh was currently working her way through her custard creams not just because it was afternoon tea time but because she was piqued. She always ate when she'd her nose out of joint and this afternoon there were three good reasons why she was in a state of annoyance.

The first was because it would seem she was the last to know Moira was expecting. Due in March no less. This bolt-from-the-blue news had seen her choke on her custard cream earlier that morning. It was the last thing she'd expected to come out of Moira's mouth.

Moira had had to smack her on the back several times and fetch her a glass of water. It had stilled the coughing but not the shock of little Moira or mouthy Moira, as she'd come to think of her in later years, becoming a mammy. She'd been certain it would be Aisling she'd be knitting for in the not too distant future.

'Does Mrs Flaherty know?' she'd asked, once the crumbs had been dislodged. This was important because she'd be even more put out if the cook had been told before her. 'Or, Ita, James and Evie?'

Moira looked cagey. You had to tread carefully with Bronagh if you wanted access to her biscuit stash. 'Mrs Flaherty does but I only told her this morning and the only reason I gave her the news before you was because I was desperate for a bacon sandwich. I haven't mentioned it to the others yet, I promise. It's too soon. I'll wait until I've a bit of bump going on.'

Bronagh was mollified because she could understand the power of a bacon sandwich. It took all her powers not to trot down the stairs of a morning for one herself. Eat your Special K, Bronagh, she'd tell herself. You'll feel much better for it. It was a lie, she knew she'd feel much better for a squidgy, greasy bacon butty. Still and all, she couldn't afford to be going out and buying a whole new wardrobe in a larger size. 'And what did she have to say?'

Moira grinned. 'What you'd expect. Feck. Quite a few times actually.' The rosy-cheeked cook might have looked as though she'd stepped straight from the pages of a children's nursery rhyme but that was where the resemblance ended. She'd a potty mouth on her at times, especially if Foxy Loxy had paid a visit overnight or the youngest O'Mara child had just announced she was pregnant.

'She also cried and said the baby was sure to be beautiful before giving me a big cuddle. I thought I was going to suffocate between her bosoms, Bronagh.'

Bronagh nodded, her face a picture of seriousness envisaging the scene.

'Then she said she'd start knitting tonight and she gave me extra bacon in my sandwich.'

Bronagh recalled how Moira had also gone on to inform her that now she was eating for two she'd need two custard creams of a morning. The one biscuit begrudgingly handed over after Moira ran through her poor student in need of a sugary boost routine of a morning would no longer cut the mustard. As such, Bronagh had better stock up.

She'd asked Moira when the wedding was because she assumed a baby went hand in hand with a big do and had been flummoxed by Moira's reaction. She'd burst into tears. This was very unlike her. She was like a walnut was Moira, a tough nut to crack. It must be down to hormones, Bronagh deduced.

She sympathised because if anybody knew about errant hormones, it was her. The menopause couldn't be all that different to pregnancy surely? With both you wound up with an enormous belly the only differences being you didn't get a hairy face at the end of one or a baby at the end of the other. She'd crossed her legs then thinking she'd prefer the hairy face.

Apparently, there was to be no wedding which was disappointing because Bronagh did enjoy a good wedding and a chance to don her glad rags, although she didn't fancy having to go into stair-climbing training again. She'd even have had a plus one to bring to it this time but Moira, when she'd wiped her eyes and scoffed the biscuits Bronagh had thrust at her, was adamant there was to be no wedding.

She'd told her what had transpired with Tom and Bronagh had offered to go round and give him a jolly good talking to amongst other things. She'd clenched her fists and looked fierce because great bottom he may have but he was behaving like a great arse in her opinion and Moira deserved better.

Moira had thought that if he were to open the door to Bronagh looking the way she did at that moment in time, he'd be terrified. She was tempted to unleash her on Tom but chewing her lip she decided scaring him into talking to her wasn't going to achieve anything. She made Bronagh promise to leave him well alone before heading out the door.

The second reason Bronagh was annoyed was because Maureen had forgotten to mention she'd put an offer in on a love nest for her and Donal. A Cape Codder no less and this was exciting news which should have come straight from the horse's mouth. Instead, she'd gleaned it second-hand from Aisling.

Yes, yes, she knew it was all pending, they'd the apartment and Donal's house to sell first but she'd have liked to have been kept abreast of the goings-on by Maureen. They were supposed to be friends after all.

She'd given her a sniffy call at lunchtime and had only warmed up towards the end of it when Maureen promised she'd be the first to know if the open home their agent was holding at Donal's that weekend was successful. They'd then whiled away twenty minutes discussing Moira and calling Tom a few choice names.

Maureen had moved on from the name calling, after calling Tom a pox bottle, to talk knitting.

She'd be in charge of cardigans and Bronagh could do hats and booties. They'd have to go with greens and yellows, of course, Bronagh said, but Maureen felt pink would be a safe bet. She could feel it in her water that Moira would have a girl.

'You sound very certain, Maureen,' Bronagh had said, nibbling on her sandwich wondering if there was something else she'd not been filled in on.

'Bronagh, I'm a firm believer that in life what goes around comes around and Moira's going to have an adorable little girl baby just like herself who will grow into a nightmare of a teenager to have her pulling her hair out. It's only fair and just.'

Bronagh had smiled at that before recalling what else had happened she'd not been a part of. 'I have to say, Maureen, I was miffed missing out on the weekend's excitement. Hollywood superstars getting up to shenanigans in room ten. Who'd have thought? I'd have liked to have been in the newspapers too given my longstanding position as receptionist here at O'Mara's.' It had been a missed opportunity to point out her long service, Bronagh thought.

'You'd a lucky escape because let me tell you, fame isn't all it's cracked up to be. Strangers keep tapping me on the shoulder and asking if I'm Maureen O'Mara and if so would I do the splits for them.' Her tone brightened. 'Although I have taken a lot of orders for the Mo-pant as a result.'

Their conversation had come to an end as a windblown Canadian couple came in, back from a morning's sightseeing, and Bronagh set about welcoming them.

Now she drummed her fingers on the desktop as she got to the fourth reason her knickers were knotty. She'd had a most unsatisfactory telephone conversation with Leonard last night. They chatted most evenings and most evenings Bronagh put the telephone down with a silly smile on her face before going through to the front room to relay all the day's news at Leonard's end to her mam.

She'd been excited when he told her he'd booked his sailing from Liverpool. This trip was to be different because for the first time Leonard would be staying with her and her mam and not at the guesthouse. She'd broached the topic with her mam before extending the invitation to Leonard.

She knew her mammy thought the sun shone out of Lenny and how much she enjoyed his company but she'd not been sure how she'd feel about her youngest child having a man friend sleeping under the family roof even if they were both long-in-the-tooth adults.

She'd braced herself for awkward questions like, 'But where will he sleep, Bronagh? In your sister's old room?' To her surprise, none had been forthcoming with her mammy saying, 'Listen Bronagh when you get to my age you've seen it all. Nothing shocks me these days.' There was a twinkle in her eye and Bronagh had been mortified at the implication.

Nevertheless, she'd be sure to call in at Marks and Spencer's to update her underwear and nighties. They were due for an overhaul and what better excuse than Leonard coming to stay.

Last night though, she'd moved the conversation on to his sister, Joan.

'I thought I might call around to see her, Lenny. Take us both a slice of cake from Cherry on Top. What do you think to that?' She'd expected him to think it a grand idea.

He didn't.

'Ah now, you don't need to be doing that, Bronagh. Sure, she's a bit of a hermit our Joan. Likes to keep herself to herself.'

Bronagh frowned, clutching the phone tighter than was necessary. 'Leonard Walsh, you sound cagey. What's the story? What aren't you telling me?'

'Not at all, Bronagh, and there's no story. She's what you'd call eccentric, my sister. I doubt you'd get a warm reception cake or no cake. She doesn't take kindly to strangers landing on the doorstep.'

'But that's just it, Leonard. I shouldn't be a stranger, should I?'

'You've a point there but listen, how about I take you around to meet her when I'm over? It's only a couple of weeks away.'

'You said that last time you were here.'

'I did but the time got away on us.'

Bronagh didn't think this was the case, they'd had plenty of time to call in on her but Leonard had changed the subject each time she'd brought it up. 'I feel as though you don't want me to meet her, Lenny.'

His hesitation confirmed her suspicions.

'Listen, Bronagh, Joan's tricky. Leave it at that would you.'

There'd been a terseness to his tone she'd not liked and she'd been feeling out of sorts ever since.

There was something Leonard wasn't sharing with her about Joan alright and Bronagh didn't like not being privy to things.

Well, she thought now, hitting a key on the Mac and watching the screen come to life, if the mountain wouldn't come to Muhammad...

Chapter Twenty-eight

Joan pulled the net curtain back an inch to see who was knocking at the door. A woman she didn't recognise was standing on the front step tugging at her skirt with one hand and holding what looked like a cake box in her other.

She let the curtain fall and hesitated because she wasn't sure as to what she should do. She was swaying towards pretending she wasn't home. It was, after all, the easier option but she was curious as to who the woman was and she'd like to know what was in the box.

Curiosity won out and Joan wound her way around all the obstacles to the hallway. She was so familiar with the clutter now that she barely registered it. She could make out the silhouette of the woman through the leaded light glass panels in the front door and she paused, what did she want?

She knocked a second time, louder this time, and Joan found her voice. 'I'm coming!' She unlocked the door, opening it only so far as was necessary, a tentative smile on her face as she said hello.

The woman's face broke into a wide smile. 'Hello, there. You must be Joan. I'm Bronagh Hanrahan.'

Joan never forgot a face and she stared at her blankly, not wanting to seem rude, but she'd no clue as to who she was. 'I'm sorry, have we met before?'

'No, we haven't but I thought it was high time we did and men are absolutely useless at that sort of thing don't you think? I'm Leonard's friend.'

Joan blinked. This was the woman who worked at the guesthouse where he chose to stay on his visits home and with whom he'd become rather more than just friends. She'd decided to take matters into her own hands and come calling. She wondered what Leonard would have to say to that. Then, remembering herself she smiled back. It was genuinely warm because she'd begun to think Bronagh was a figment of her brother's imagination and now here she was in the flesh on her doorstep.

Bronagh held the box up. 'I've bought us cake, can I come in? I thought it would be lovely if we could get to know one another a little better.' Nobody had ever accused Bronagh of being too subtle.

Joan's gaze flitted to the box longingly. She'd a sweet tooth when it came to cake and the likes and it was nearly time for her afternoon cup of tea. It would be nice to have company.

For Bronagh's part, she took in Leonard's younger sister deciding she'd no clue what he'd been on about her being a hermit. Sure, everybody knew hermits had long straggly hair and a wild look to them. She threw in a few missing teeth too for good measure and a hermit would have peeped out the window, not come to the door smiling like so.

Mind you she did have a tight grip on the door Bronagh thought, noticing her white knuckles. From the little she could see, Joan was a tad frumpy given she wasn't all that much older than Bronagh. She'd a full set of teeth on her though but she'd let her hair go grey. It was pulled back into a bun and the silver threads were what Bronagh aspired to one day. Not yet though sure, she was too young to be doing away with the hair colour just yet.

She put a hand to her own black-brown hair knowing she was due to get her roots retouched. She was looking a little like Sally the Skunk and she'd have to sort it before Leonard arrived.

Joan would've been a pretty girl in her day and her smile lit up her face but even when she smiled there was a sadness to her. It was there in her eyes Bronagh thought, trying not to stare. She was very intuitive when it came to getting the measure of people. It came from years of dealing with guests from all walks of life at the guesthouse. There was a hole inside of Joan and she'd like to find out why.

She took a step forward expecting her to open the door and usher her in hospitably but a sudden change came over her. It was as if she'd pulled the shutters down.

'Are you alright?' Bronagh asked peering at her.

For a moment Joan had forgotten her home was out of bounds to the outside world. Nobody had crossed the threshold apart from Leonard in years. She wasn't a silly woman, she knew how the way she lived would be perceived by others and if she hadn't then Leonard had made sure she did.

Joan's jaw tightened, knowing an explanation would be expected as to why Bronagh wasn't being welcomed in. What could she say? She doubted too that Leonard knew she was planning on calling to see her and he wouldn't be best pleased when he found out she had.

'Joan?' Bronagh asked once more, wondering what on earth the problem was.

'I'm sorry, Bronagh, the cake was a lovely idea but it's not a good time I'm afraid.'

'Oh, have you guests?' Bronagh's feet were planted firmly on the ground; she'd no intention of being sent on her way. 'Because I've plenty to go round.' The wedge of cake could be cut into thirds or quarters if need be. Her gut was telling her there was nobody else here though. That there'd been nobody else here for quite some time. Something was amiss.

'Erm, no. It's not that.' Joan hastily tried to formulate an excuse. 'I, er, I erm, decided to give the old place a long-overdue going over today and I've turned it upside down I'm afraid. It's a mess so it is. I'd be embarrassed for you to see it like so.' She made to close the door and Bronagh all but stuck her foot in the gap.

'Well you've no need to be,' she laughed. 'You want to see the state some of our guests leave their rooms. There's nothing could shock me.' She mimicked her mam's words when she'd told her about Leonard coming to stay. 'Besides how could you say no to mud cake with chocolate ganache *and* whipped cream?' She'd decided to play it safe with chocolate cake because everybody liked chocolate cake.

Joan's mouth watered despite herself. Bronagh seemed very nice if a little pushy. Not the sort to judge at any rate. Could she trust her? She wanted to.

Bronagh smiled encouragingly and Joan found herself stepping away from the door so as she could let her brother's lady friend come in. Her heart was pounding and she'd gone clammy but it was too late now Bronagh had stepped inside and Joan closed the door behind her.

The first thing that hit Bronagh was the smell. She couldn't pinpoint what it was other than to say it made her think of decaying fruit. She sensed Joan's keen eyes on her and she forced herself to swallow her shock.

Leonard's reasons for not wanting to bring her here had become crystal clear. In all her days she'd never seen anything quite like what she was surrounded with now. There was stuff everywhere. Boxes were piled on top of boxes, newspapers and magazines stacked high next to books and that was just here in the hallway. It was a hovel.

She managed to keep her expression neutral however because she'd come this far and she'd not be leaving now.

Joan avoided eye contact with Bronagh, making apologetic noises about the mess before squeezing down the narrows gaps in the hall and disappearing into the kitchen. Bronagh tried to keep up, panicking she'd be swallowed up by the mayhem surrounding her never to be heard of again.

She emerged into the kitchen instantly being hit by the smell. It was stronger in here and she tracked its source to the bags of rubbish piled up by the back door. She made a quick sweep of the place taking in the sink filled with dirty dishes and table bowed under the weight of the things piled upon it. The only clear place in the entire kitchen was the window sill.

Joan set to moving things around so as Bronagh could sit down and when she was seated she picked up the various tins of food and shifted them into the middle of the table to clear space.

'There,' she said glancing to Bronagh anxiously. 'I'll make the tea.'

'Shall I be mother and cut the cake?' Bronagh asked, the box on her lap.

'No, no, I can manage thank you.' Joan took it from her and sought a space to rest it down. She'd enjoyed playing hostess once upon a time.

The chaos in which Joan lived was like an elephant in the room and Bronagh skirted around it as she chattered on about the recent scandal that had rocked Hollywood and O'Mara's inadvertent part in it all.

All the while, she watched Joan from beneath her lashes as she bustled about. Despite the bedlam of her kitchen and presumably the rest of the house, she seemed to know where everything was and was in her element humming softly as she busied herself.

Bronagh took the opportunity to scan the space, her eyes moving over the mountains of things Joan had piled up around her. It must have taken years for things to get to this point, she mused. It can't have always been like this either. She wondered when it had begun. Was it a cry for attention because she was lonely?

Bronagh recalled having read something or seen something on the television, she couldn't remember which, about people who lived like this. Hoarding it was called. It was an illness which often had its roots in a trauma of some sorts. They couldn't help themselves.

She wondered what Jane's trauma was and why Leonard allowed her to live like this. Apart from anything else, it was unsanitary.

She resolved there and then as she breathed through her mouth to see beyond the mess to the woman who lived here.

She wouldn't turn her nose up at someone with a physical illness and indeed hadn't when faced with the care of her mam. This was a different sort of sickness altogether but it was one she was certain Joan hadn't willingly chosen to be afflicted with. She deserved her compassion and if she'd let her, her help.

Despite her resolution not to sit in judgment, for the first time ever, Bronagh wasn't looking forward to tucking into her slice of the gooey cake.

Where on earth would Joan locate any clean cups and saucers let alone side plates? she thought, noting the dirty dishes piled in the sink and spilling over onto the worktop.

She willed herself not to dwell on what might be sniffing around under all those rubbish bags over by the door, attracted by the food scraps.

To her surprise, Joan carved a path over to the sideboard upon which an assortment of ugly old Toby jugs resided and, opening the cupboards, she retrieved a china tea set on a gleaming silver tray. She also managed to procure two side plates and a cake stand along with a server.

'I've never had a reason to use these before,' Joan said, looking pleased and carrying the tray over to the worktop as the kettle began to boil. She dropped two teabags into the pretty teapot. 'It's Noritake.'

Bronagh smiled and murmured, 'Lovely.' She was unsure whether Joan was referring to the china or the tea and didn't want to appear ignorant.

She finished her task and carried the tray over to the table, the cups rattling in their saucers as she placed it down.

'I'm gasping, thank you, Joan.'

Joan smiled, beginning to relax and enjoy herself as the minutes ticked by with Bronagh making no mention of anything being untoward about her unconventional way of life. She'd warmed to her and thought Leonard had done well for himself with the receptionist.

She slid the cake onto the stand and brought it over to the table, admiring the rich, buttercream swirls on top; it was a squeeze but she managed to make room.

'I'll cut it, shall I?' Joan looked to Bronagh for confirmation.

'Grand.'

She sliced into the deep triangle. 'This looks delicious. I can't remember the last time I had a slice of chocolate cake.' The two halves were distributed onto the plates which Bronagh noticed matched the teacups as she poured hers and Joan's tea. She couldn't echo Joan's sentiment. There wasn't a week went by without a slice of chocolate cake passing her lips.

'Bon appétit,' Joan said, picking up her silver fork and digging in.

Bronagh echoed the sentiment, thinking what a strange tableau the pair of them must make sitting here in this midden eating cake in a perfectly civilised manner.

Chapter Twenty-nine

To Bronagh's amazement, two hours had passed since she'd arrived at Joan's. She'd almost forgotten about her surroundings as they got to know one another.

She and Joan discovered, once they'd devoured their cake and were sipping on their tea that they had common ground and lots of it. Neither of them had ever married although they'd both come close. Joan had cared for her poorly dad just as Bronagh still cared for her mam.

Bronagh gave Joan a thoughtful once-over deciding if they were to be friends, and she sensed they were, then there was no point holding back. With this in mind, she began at the beginning of her story when her mam had finally received a diagnosis of ME, a complex and at times disabling chronic fatigue illness, after years of people thinking it was all in her head or, putting it down to nerves.

'I've an older sister Hilary, who's married with children, something she likes to remind me of at any given opportunity. Actually, they're not children anymore either, they've flown the nest and are off doing their own thing. When our mam took ill though they were young and it fell to me to take care of her. I didn't mind because we got on well Mam and I. Besides, I wouldn't hear of her going into a nursing home or the like.' She shook her dark head vehemently. 'No, that would have been the end of her.'

Joan interrupted sitting forward in her seat. 'I know what you mean. Our dad smoked all his life. He loved it so he did. Mam used to say he'd eat the bloody things if he could. It caught up with him in the end though and he wound up on oxygen barely able to manage himself. I'd have had to arrange for the house to be sold if Dad were to go into care. I hated the thought of him leaving his home so, I cut back my hours at the bookkeepers where I worked as a secretary and moved back to look after him.'

'Leonard would have been away at sea,' Bronagh said.

Joan nodded. 'Yes, he was a stranger to me for many years after he joined the navy. He had the wanderlust did Leonard.' She didn't add that her brother had never fully appreciated what she'd done for their dad in those last few years. He'd no clue what was involved in looking after him. Perhaps if he'd an inkling he'd be kinder to her.

'It always falls to one,' Bronagh said, reaching over and patting Joan's hand, assuming the sadness etched on her face had been brought on by talking about her father.

Joan nodded her agreement then asked, 'You said you nearly married?'

'I did, yes. It was a long time ago now. Kevin was his name and I fell for him good and proper. There was always Mam though but Kevin didn't seem to mind, or at least that's what I thought. We were engaged and I felt I was the luckiest woman alive because he wasn't just good to me he was good to Mam too. Then one day he turned around and said he couldn't marry someone who'd always put him second. It broke my heart but you don't die of a broken heart now do you?'

Joan nodded her agreement.

'So, I picked myself up and carried on because that's what you have to do.'

Joan agreed. Her mind was drifting back to Owen, the man she'd thought she'd marry. She began to talk.

Joan – 1965

Terrence Walsh's keen eyes watched his daughter from where he sat hunched in his chair. Chester was watching her too, he saw with a fond glance at the old dog, who was on his last legs just like himself. He reached down and gave him a scratch behind the ear.

Joan was humming as she set out the tea things. It gave him a boost to watch her flitting about happy. She'd invited a chap she'd been stepping out with to tea which was a turn-up indeed and the reason for her humming.

It was a joyous sound because to Terence's mind Joan hadn't been happy for a long time. Her childhood had been marred by the fire. It had affected her deeply and both he and Maggie always felt it had changed their daughter. They'd no clue as to how to get the carefree child who skipped home from school with news of her day back though. It had been of great sadness to them both.

She'd grown into a rebellious teenager and then one day the stomping up the stairs and banging of her bedroom door had stopped. At first, they'd put it down to her having a falling out with that friend of hers, Brigid. They were thick as thieves those two but as time went on Joan had retreated into herself and they'd felt sure there was more to it than her having words with her pal. They'd never gotten to the bottom of it; Joan would clam up if her mam asked her what the matter was.

Maggie had tentatively broached the subject of Joan and what to do about her with the family doctor once. What a waste of time that had been. He's said some people were predisposed to be melancholy. It was all to do with chemicals in the brain he'd said, and if they felt she was a danger to herself then there were places that could help with that.

Maggie thought about the austere, Grangegorman Mental Hospital locked away behind gates and stared at the doctor in horror. She'd not send her daughter to an institution.

He and Maggie had decided there was nothing for it but to accept Joan the way she was. It was just her way they concluded, trying not to worry as their friends' children began to move on, marrying and starting families.

There'd been a time he and Maggie had wondered whether Joan might choose the Church. The life of a nun would've suited her with its day-to-day orderliness. Mind you, they'd never have let her bring all her bits and pieces with her. The state of her room had driven her poor mam mad; you could barely get in the door she'd that much stuff.

Joan had gotten on well enough in her schooling though and when she'd finished she'd enrolled in secretarial college. They'd had high hopes for her then. Doors would open for her. She'd make new friends. The world would be her oyster when she qualified. Sure, who was to say she might not decide to travel like Leonard had? Hadn't the Blakes' girl, Susan, just set sail for Canada? Who was to say their Joanie wouldn't follow suit and as much as they didn't want to wave her off, they did want her to grasp hold of life and move out of the rut she seemed to be in.

Instead, Joan took a position in a small bookkeeping firm off Dame Street. It suited her well enough and she'd spread her wings a little by moving into a tidy one-bedroom flat on the north side of the river.

Then, when Maggie had passed suddenly a few years, back it had only been a matter of months before he'd become as good as useless. Joan, God bless her, had cut her hours back at the office to look after him. It wasn't what he'd wanted for her but he couldn't look after himself and he hadn't wanted a stranger taking care of him. She looked after him well, too. She'd have made a grand nurse he thought.

This would be the first time she'd invited a fella home for him to meet which signalled it was serious. Terence was surprised by the pang that passed through him for his Maggie. He wished she was still here sitting in the chair next to him. He would have given anything for her to meet this Owen too and hear her take on him. Maggie would pass verdict on whether he was good enough for their girl.

'I wish your mam was still here, Joanie,' he rasped. The cigarettes he'd enjoyed for the best part of his life had taken their toll and the oxygen tank burbled away on his right. A reminder of a habit he'd no idea he'd pay so dearly for down the track.

Joan paused in her folding of a serviette. She was making them into swans. Her mam had shown her how when she was a child and, like riding a bike, the intricate folding had come back to her as soon as she'd picked up the paper napkin.

Maggie Walsh had been one for a properly set table, especially if company was coming. She'd be proud of Joan's efforts.

'I miss her too, Dad. I'd have liked her to meet Owen but I like to think she's watching over us.'

Terence nodded. He liked to think so too.

He hoped this Owen fella was a keeper because he wouldn't be here much longer and the last time Leonard had written he'd been in a South American port somewhere. His boy had been away forever, or at least it seemed that way at times. He was a wanderer that son of his, which was all well and good but he hated to think of Joanie all alone in the world. It would be of great comfort to him when he reached the pearly gates to know she'd met someone to look after her. He could go and greet his Maggie and tell her Joan would be alright. He didn't think it was too much to ask for her to at last find happiness.

'Tell me again, Joanie, how did you meet your young man?'

Joan laughed. 'Dad, he's in his thirties as am I. I'd hardly say he's my young man.'

Terence flapped his hand impatiently.

'I met him in the park walking Chester. It was Chester who introduced us because he took a fancy to Owen's dog, Lucy.'

'What sort of a name is Lucy for a dog?'

'Owen's a big fan of Lucille Ball. And it was the most energetic I'd seen Chester for a long time.' She grinned and to Terence's eyes, she looked like a child again.

He chortled at the story and patted the dog's head once more. There was life in the old boy yet!

'And why's he never married?'

'Dad!'

'I can ask him if you like,' Terence wheezed, a cheeky glint in his eyes.

'Don't you dare. He's never married because he's never met anyone he cared to spend the rest of his life with. It's a perfectly good reason and one I can relate to myself.'

'Until now.'

'You'll scare him off if you come out with talk like that,' Joan said, setting her paper swan down and going into the kitchen to check on the joint of beef she had cooking. The smell of gently roasting meat was tantalising.

'Joan, the door!' Terence called ten minutes later to his daughter, who was upstairs tidying herself up. She skipped down the stairs as she had as a child and Terence sat up in his chair a little straighter as he heard the door open.

Present Day

'Dad thought the sun rose and set with Owen,' Joan said with a faraway look in her eyes. 'I did too.' Her sigh was weighty. 'But we weren't meant to be.'

Joan's story had ended somewhat abruptly and Bronagh assumed Joan's Owen had walked away for the same reasons Kevin had. He couldn't take there being three in their relationship.

Joan turned her gaze to Bronagh then. 'Do you believe in fate and that things happen for a reason?'

Bronagh was thoughtful, taking a moment before replying. 'I believe God has a path for each of us and that it might not be one we want to take but we have to have faith and follow it.'

Joan wasn't sure she agreed because she'd lost her faith after what had happened to her on that long-ago night. She did believe in fate though. Perhaps it was fate had brought Bronagh to her door this afternoon. The muscle in her jaw twitched as she pondered whether Bronagh would think her ridiculous if she asked her advice over the invitation that had been plaguing her. She'd yet to slip a note through Gordon's letterbox with her apologies explaining she couldn't make tea after all.

Bronagh glanced at her watch and her eyes widened. The afternoon had disappeared! It was time she was off or she'd miss the butchers on her way home and she'd planned to call in and get some of Neville's juicy lamb chops. 'Joan, I've so enjoyed our chat but I've got to be off or the butcher's will be closed and me and Mam will be having cheese on toast for our tea.' She got up from her chair and slung her bag over her shoulder.

Joan opened her mouth and closed it again, having decided that no, Bronagh would think her foolish stewing over a harmless invitation that was hardly an offer of marriage merely tea.

The indecision on Joan's face didn't escape Bronagh's wily eyes. 'What is it?'

'It's nothing. I've thoroughly enjoyed meeting you too.'

'Nothing is usually something.'

'I don't want to hold you up.'

'Sure, there's nothing wrong with cheese on toast if you've stale bread in need of using and a sharp cheddar in and I've both so come on then.'

'It's advice I'm after and I'm afraid you'll think I'm an old fool when I tell you what has me bothered.'

'I'll think no such thing. Out with it.'

It poured out in a gush. Gordon, the way in which they'd chat companionably each Friday and how she knew he was lonely since his wife had passed. 'It's the company he misses, as do I. I'd like to go for tea but I can't.'

'Why not?' Bronagh frowned. 'Because I think you should definitely go. He's your friend, Joan. Don't push him away.'

'I can't go because invitations have to be reciprocated and I'm in no position to do so, now am I?' Joan waved her arm around the place, nearly knocking a tin off its precarious position atop a box. It was the first time the state of the house had been alluded to since Bronagh got here other than Joan's brief explanation as to having decided to give the place a going over.

Tears pricked Joan's eyes and what started as a drip turned into a landslide.

Bronagh bustled around the table and wrapped an arm around her. She recognised hopelessness when she saw it and was filled with annoyance toward Leonard. He'd bought sunshine into her life but he'd let his sister down.

Well, he might have been happy to pretend her illness didn't exist by staying elsewhere and keeping his visits short but she was no ostrich. She'd already decided to pay a visit to the local library to try to find out more about Joan's condition and see what help could be sought.

'Oh, Joan. It's all too much on your own isn't it?' she said now.

Joan nodded, sniffing. She pulled away embarrassed. She kept a lid on her emotions and not even Lenny had been a party to them. She kept so much of herself hidden from view and buried beneath the things she surrounded herself with.

'I'd like to help if you'll let me.'

Could she allow someone in?

Chapter Thirty

Joan

Joan closed the door on Bronagh. She'd made a friend today. She felt lighter and knew it was down to hope. She wasn't going to have to do whatever came next on her own.

Fate had seen fit to send her brother's lady friend to her door and in doing so had offered her a hand. The choice as to whether she grasped that hand and allowed it to pull her up out of the mire she'd been living in was hers to make and she was determined she'd take Bronagh's hand with both of hers.

She needed to lay her ghosts to rest. Banish them once and for all, Owen included. She picked her way through to the front room and dug around until she found what she was looking for. It was a photograph of her dad and Owen that she'd taken with Dad's box brownie.

It had made her dad happy when one day, out of the blue, she'd asked if he minded her borrowing his old camera. He hadn't of course and she'd begun to disappear for hours on end to capture what she saw around her on film. She'd regained her passion for their shared love of photography.

She'd a keen eye, like him, her dad had said, and she'd compiled hundreds of photos of her own which she'd intended to submit to a publishing house.

Unlike her dad, she'd wanted to take her love of photography to the next level. She'd wanted to turn it from a hobby into a profession. She'd dreamed of the pictures she spent her weekends snapping, and capturing life in all its rawness as it played out on the streets of her home city, being compiled into a book.

She'd plans to submit her photographs to a publishing house but after Owen, she'd not done it. After Owen, to her dad's dismay, she'd stopped taking photographs once more. To Joan it had seemed pointless. Everything had seemed a waste of time.

She touched her fingers to her dear dad's face. Oh, how she missed him. Leonard had always found her closeness to her father hard. He'd felt pushed out, having no interest in photography himself and no shared pastime they could enjoy together. Perhaps that was why he'd opted for the navy and sailed far away from them all. She hadn't meant to make him feel like that but it made his simmering anger towards her understandable.

As for Owen, the hurt didn't stab at her like it used to. She did wonder what had become of him. Whether he'd met someone else and married. She'd no clue because after he broke things off she'd never seen him again.

She used to think she'd let him down. But maybe that wasn't the case. Maybe, by not taking the time to understand why she struggled with the intimate side of their relationship, he'd let her down.

If he'd gone slower, tried to talk to her about it, even suggested she seek help... with him by her side she was certain she could have overcome her fear. He'd done none of those things though. Instead, he'd flung at her that she was frigid and if she couldn't fulfil her part in their marriage fully, what was the point?

She'd never told anyone the truth of what happened. She knew her dad blamed himself, his illness, for having put Owen off and she hated herself for not putting him right but how could she?

'This stops now, Joan,' she said out loud. 'I'm sorry, Dad. I should have trusted in you and Mum. I should've told you the truth of what happened after the circus. It's too late now though and I can't live in the past anymore.'

She put the photo back where she'd found it feeling a surge of energy as she set about compiling her photographs. She'd take them to show Gordon when she went for tea because she would go. He was a learned fellow and she'd ask for his opinion as to what she should do with them. She'd cross the bridge of a return invitation when she came to it because she was certain now that with Bronagh's help things could get better.

Chapter Thirty-one

Maureen rapped on the door before inhaling deeply all the way down into her tummy. She'd her hands at her sides, fingers pointing down as she did the mountain pose growing-out-the-top-of-her-head thing Rosi had taught her. She'd done it in the mirror once and reckoned it added a centimetre to her stature.

It was worth doing now when she wanted to be imposing. It was very hard for a short woman to be imposing. Another week had ticked by without Tom and Moira having spoken and she'd had enough. It was time to take matters into her own hands.

As the seconds ticked by, she wondered if she should adopt the proud warrior pose instead because that would have Tom thinking on when he opened the door. Rosi said she didn't need to pull the fierce face when she struck the stance but she found it helped her get in the swing of things. She was pleased she hadn't, as the door opened and a tall, spotty man she didn't know gazed down at her. She shrank back down to her normal stature under his gaze.

He had to be one of the flatmates Moira was forever moaning on about she decided, giving him the head to toe. 'Hello there, I'm wondering if Tom's about.'

She frowned as yer man barely acknowledged her, twisting his head to yell up the stairs. 'Tom, there's someone to see you.'

He wouldn't be much cop as a doctor, not with those manners she thought as he disappeared into a room off to the left leaving the door wide open.

Maureen took the opportunity to appraise the hall. A bicycle was propped up against the wall and a pair of muddy boots sat just inside the door. The clue to it being a rented property lay in the lack of adornment on the walls save for the coat hook upon which dangled a solitary rain jacket.

She did the mountain thing again trying to imagine she was Kilimanjaro as she waited.

Tom appeared at the top of the stairs and even from that distance, Maureen could see he'd paled at the sight of her. As well he should, she thought.

'Hello, Maureen. I didn't expect to see you.' He waivered there looking like he was about to turn tail and run.

She swallowed down the, 'No, I bet you jolly well didn't,' response. She'd come here with the intention of being a reasonable adult and reasonable she'd be. Unless he failed to see things her way. Then he'd find out just how unreasonable she could be.

She waited while he dragged his feet down to where she was waiting.

'How're you, Tom? I thought it was time you and I had a little chat.'

Tom licked his lips and she could tell by his pained expression he'd rather be anywhere than where he was at that moment. Well tough, Maureen thought. He knew her well enough by now to know she wouldn't be going anywhere until she'd had her say.

You'd better come on in, Maureen. It's too cold to be standing out there.'

It was, and Maureen shivered in her lightweight jacket. She'd not wanted to acknowledge the end of their Indian summer and abrupt descent into autumn hence the unseasonal outfit. From heatwave to arctic temperatures within the space of days, that was Ireland for you, she thought, grateful to step inside to the centrally heated warmth.

Tom shut the door behind her and ushered her into the kitchen.

It wasn't too bad a place considering they were students, Maureen thought, checking the space out. In fact, she saw, noting the clean worktop and neatly lined bin, it was positively shipshape and she was sure she could smell disinfectant. Then she remembered they were medical students. That explained it. Medicine was a serious business, so. They were bound to be hygienic it went with the territory.

'Here we are, Maureen.' Tom pulled a chair out for her. 'Please, have a seat.'

Maureen nearly wept at his good manners. It was the waiter in him, she thought. Then, she remembered he'd hardly been behaving like a gentleman this past week and sat down with her lips pressed together.

'Would you like a cup of tea?'

'Grand,' Maureen answered in a clipped tone.

'How's Moira?' Tom asked as he flicked the kettle on and set about making their tea.

'You remember who she is then? Your pregnant girlfriend.'

Tom glanced over, a wounded look on his face. 'I suppose I deserved that.'

Maureen didn't say anything. Lovely manners he may have but she wasn't going to make this easy for him. He'd some explaining to do treating her daughter the way he had.

He went back to what he was doing and when he'd made their brews he carried them over to the table. 'There's some biscuits somewhere,' he said, placing Maureen's in front of her and looking past her to the pantry cupboard.

'I don't need a biscuit, Tom. Sit down.'

He did as he was told, pulling out a chair across the table from her. His fingers drummed anxiously on the timber top and Maureen didn't need to look under the table to know his leg would be jiggling too.

'Now then, why don't you tell me what's going on with you?' She stared him down. He was a handsome fella was Tom and Maureen had him down as a good fella too. She'd be staying put until they sorted things out because she was a firm believer there was nothing that couldn't be fixed. It might not be put back together the way it had been but it could still be mended so he and Moira could move forward.

Tom stropped the drumming and picked up his mug; his hand shook a little and he put it back down again, staying silent.

'Are you scared of settling down, is that it? You wouldn't be the first man with a fear of commitment. But you know these are modern times we live in, son, and I haven't come here today to twist your arm to make an honest woman of Moira.'

'I know that,' he mumbled, but didn't look up.

'You don't have to share the rest of your life with her. You don't even have to be in a relationship with her if you don't want to but you do need to decide on the role you're going to play in your child's life.'

'But I want to be with Moira.' Tom looked lost as he stared across the table at Maureen.

'Just not with a baby, is that it?'

He nodded.

Maureen's sigh was weighty. 'Well, Tom, I'm sorry to hear that because you don't have a choice. If you stay with Moira she's going to come as a package and if you don't then you'll have to take responsibility for what's happened and work out how you're going to play things between the pair of you. Do you understand?'

Her tone brooked no argument and Tom nodded.

'She's been beside herself this week, I'll have you know. It's been an annus horribilis week so it has.' Maureen was comfortable using her new favourite catchphrase around Tom given he was a man of medicine. He'd not be thinking rude things like Rosi had.

Despite him being a man of medicine, Tom still glanced up sharply at Maureen's turn of phrase. It was the sort of thing he and Moira would have a laugh about.

He missed her badly and had wanted to run after her when she'd walked out on him that Friday night but his feet had been rooted to the ground. It had been a shock. He'd not seen what she'd had to say coming and knew he'd not behaved well.

He'd thought about calling her so as they could talk things through but he hadn't known what it was he wanted to say. His head had been all over the place. It still was.

He'd no idea what he was going to do for money now either, given he was officially unemployed but he'd not felt he could show his face in Quinn's, not with the way things stood between him and Moira. It would have put Quinn and Aisling in an impossible situation.

He ran his hands through his hair. It was getting too long. He'd have to get it cut but that could wait for another day.

'It's a scary thing having a baby,' Maureen said. 'I remember when Pat arrived and the enormity of me and Brian being responsible for this little person overwhelmed me. I was sure I was going to drop him or the like.'

There was no need to mention she had, in fact, dropped him because, sure she'd picked him up and dusted him off and he'd been right as rain. Although, she had worried about the twitch he'd developed not long after. You worried about everything with babies and nine times out of ten what had you pulling your hair out passed soon enough and they were on to the next thing like refusing the lovely stewed apple you'd made for them. He'd been a fussy little fellow so he had.

Tom's head was tilted to one side. 'It's more than being scared, Maureen. I'm terrified.'

She could see he wanted to say more. 'I'm listening, son.'

He studied the back of his hands which he'd laid flat on the table. 'There's four of us kids in the family but there should have been five. I'd a brother who died when he was fifteen months old. Aidan. He was born with Batten disease. It's complicated but there's a one in four chance of a child being born with it if both parents carry the defective gene which my parents did. We all watched Aidan struggle away until it was a blessing when he passed and didn't have to suffer anymore. It's why I chose to study to be a doctor. I want to stop people suffering.' He looked across to Maureen. 'My parents didn't know they were carriers. What if I am? What if Moira is? What if the baby's born sick?'

'Ah, Tom.' Maureen got up and moved around the table. She pulled out the chair next to him and sat down putting her hand on top of his. 'It was a terrible thing for your poor brother and your family to go through. Unimaginable. But, you can't let what happened dictate your life. You have to be brave because if you hold yourself back and don't dive in you'll never know how wonderful it can be.'

'But what if...?'

'What if this baby is the best thing that ever happened to you and Moira? How do you know he or she won't be? You don't. I can't guarantee it either way just like I can't tell you you won't have heartache along the way. No one can because it's called living.'

Tom was silent for a minute and the only sound was the clock on the wall ticking. 'You're good, do you know that?' he said finally.

Maureen smiled. 'I've four of my own, Tom. I've plenty of practice when it comes to talking sense into you young ones. So, will you tell her what you just told me?'

He nodded.

'Come on then, fetch your coat. There's no time like the present. I'll drop you off myself,' Maureen said, getting up. She wasn't going to risk Tom backing out by saying he'd drive himself. She happened to know Moira was currently working her way through a packet of biscuits at home and Aisling was spending some much-needed quality time with Quinn.

'Maureen, can we make a pit stop on the way? There's something I need to get.'

'Flowers?'

'No, I've something else in mind. Something that's more Moira.'

Chapter Thirty-two

Maureen dropped Tom off at O'Mara's with an encouraging smile. It was his lucky day insomuch as Bronagh wasn't working, being Saturday. She was loyal was Bronagh and he wouldn't have made it through the guesthouse's reception area unscathed had she been on the front desk.

Tom managed to greet James in a normal voice despite his anxiousness.

James watched him go, wondering why he had a stuffed toy behind his back. He didn't think Rosi was in town with Noah. The phone ringing distracted him and he forgot all about Tom as he took a booking for a couple from Tipperary.

Tom took the stairs two at a time, eager to see Moira despite his nerves at how he'd be received. He tapped on the door and then fidgeted like he had when he was a schoolboy who'd been sent to see the principal while he waited for her to answer. He knew she was home.

Maureen had said Moira had a day on the sofa watching mindless television omnibuses planned. Aisling was out, for which he was grateful because he knew how the O'Mara sisters banded together and he'd be in for a lynching were she in, or a tongue lashing at the very least.

He blinked as Moira suddenly appeared. She'd wrenched the door open with an annoyed expression on her pretty face at having being interrupted in the middle of her soap. She'd a cracker in her hand which also annoyed her because she'd chowed her way through all the nice stuff and was now onto dry crackers.

At the sight of Tom staring uncertainly at her, the cracker snapped sending a smattering of crumbs floating to the ground.

Why did he have to show up now when she was the poster girl for Saturday slothfulness?

She'd not bothered getting dressed today, not seeing any point. She knew she'd a tea stain down the front of her pyjama top and her hair was a bird's nest. When she'd pictured this moment, and she had at least one hundred times, she'd been fully made-up in a skintight little number to show him what he was missing.

For Tom's part, he thought her a sight for sore eyes.

Moira rallied herself and made to close the door in his face. She'd some pride left and wasn't going to make this easy for him. Tom stuck his foot in the door though and from behind his back, he produced a soft toy. 'I brought you this. Foxy Loxy,' he said, thrusting it at her.

Moira took it, tears springing unbidden at the gesture. She hid them by inspecting the stuffed animal. Any normal fella would have brought flowers but not Tom, he'd brought her a cuddly toy and not just any toy, a fox because he knew she loved O'Mara's fox. This was what she loved most about Tom. He wasn't like other fellas. Just last night she'd hung out the window as Foxy Loxy had done one of his danger-run raids. She'd whispered down to him that she was miserable and liked to think she'd seen sympathy glowing in his eyes as he stared up at her, half-snaffled sausage clamped between his pointy little teeth.

'Moira, please... I know you don't owe me anything but would you hear me out for a few minutes?'

Moira didn't say anything but she stepped aside so he could come in.

Tom followed her through to the living room and she gestured for him to sit at the table keeping things formal. He glanced over at the sofa, spying the empty biscuit packet and mug on the coffee table along with the pillow and blanket on the sofa. She'd clearly taken up residence there today he deduced. He wondered how she'd been keeping.

There was no offer of a drink of any sort and Tom sat opposite Moira who was holding her toy Foxy Loxy to her.

'Why've you come now, Tom?' She was angry he'd made her wait this long. It had been, well it had been annus horribilis. She didn't say this though as she waited for his reply.

'Because of your mammy.'

'What?'

'Maureen called around to see me.'

'Oh, I see. Did she threaten to take you out if you didn't come and talk to me?' Moira was only half joking.

Tom's mouth twitched. 'Not quite. But she did make me see what an eejit I've been.'

'I'd have said arse.'

'Fair play.'

'There's a reason I've been acting like a—'

'An arse.'

'Arse.'

'Go on then, tell me.'

Tom took a deep breath and told Moira his fears.

Moira clutched Foxy Loxy tightly. She'd expected a speech on why he wasn't ready to be a dad and was unprepared for what he'd said. 'Why've you never mentioned your brother to me before?' Her heart was aching for his lost brother, for Tom and his family.

'I don't like to talk about it.' He shook his head, his hair now pulled back into a ponytail at the nape of his neck. 'And I should have told you, I know that, but I didn't want to scare you either.'

Moira stared at him seeing the vulnerability plastered to his face. 'I don't scare easily.' This wasn't true, she was still petrified at the thought of becoming a mammy but what Tom had just said hadn't changed how she felt. 'I want this baby. I won't change my mind and if history repeated itself with that terrible illness, well, I'd be heartbroken, of course, I would, but I'm strong, Tom. Stronger than you think.'

He eyed her for a moment. 'I know you are.'

'Besides, the odds would be extremely low of us both carrying the gene. You know that. You're a doctor.'

He knew that on a rational level but on an emotional level it was murky waters. He said as much.

'Life is one big unknown.' Moira shrugged and then pointed to her tummy. 'None of us knows what it's going to dish up. I didn't expect this to happen but it has and I'm going to do my best by this little one.'

Tom was beginning to suspect Moira and Maureen had been binge-watching *Oprah* on account of all the wise things they were coming out with but he knew they were right. 'Will you let me be part of things?'

Moira exhaled. 'Part of the baby's life?' It was something at least.

'Yes, and yours. I don't want to lose you, Moira.'

Moira put Foxy Loxy on the table and reached across to clasp Tom's hands in her own. 'You really are an arse. You're not going to lose me. I love you, Tom.'

'I've missed you.'

'And, I've missed you. I kept going to tell you something and then I'd remember. It's been—'

'An annus horribilis week.' Tom nodded his agreement.

Moira looked startled and then remembered Mammy had hot-footed it around to his place and she grinned. 'Exactly.'

Tom pushed his chair back and strode around the table to scoop Moira up. She relaxed into his burly arms and rested her head against his chest, breathing in the scent of him for a moment. She didn't want him to ever let her go.

'We'll be okay, you know,' she mumbled into his chest. 'It won't be easy but we can do this. Mammy and Ash will help out so we can juggle everything.'

'I'll qualify in another couple of years. I won't be a student doctor forever. And, my mam and dad will help out too.'

'See, we'll be grand, and if we both try our hardest to be the best mammy and daddy we can be then our little one will be grand too, do you hear me, Tom Daly?'

'I hear you, Moira O'Mara.'

Moira grabbed hold of Tom's backside then and raised her head to seal the deal with a kiss.

Chapter Thirty-three
Two weeks to go...

Yvonne stood by her whiteboard at the front of what served as her classroom in the community centre. The room with the chairs she'd not long set out was slowly beginning to fill up. The Thursday evening four-week-long antenatal course ran throughout the year and this group was three weeks in. They were a bit of a motley crew she mused, glancing over those that were already seated.

Yvonne liked to think of herself as a fun sort of a person and she enjoyed keeping her ladies and their partners guessing by wearing a different coloured waistcoat each session.

She was the female equivalent of Joseph and his technicoloured dream coat, only in a two-tone waistcoat. Tonight's was purple with a green silk back. It was one of her favourites. Last week she'd worn the orange and navy and the week before the mustard and peach. She stitched the waistcoats herself and was proud of being not just a seasoned midwife but an avant-garde waistcoat designer too.

The table in front of her had all sorts of paraphernalia on it, ranging from the TENS machine she was going to demonstrate this evening to a stack of cloth nappies as well as a pile of disposables for those who were challenged when it came to the art of nappy folding. She'd also one of those lifelike newborn dolls lying naked as the day it was born on the table. Personally speaking, Yvonne found the boy doll a tad disturbing with its beady eyes but needs must and it fitted the bill for the nappy practising with its correct body parts.

She was expecting a full group tonight even though some of her ladies were getting close to their due dates. She greeted the last of the straggling couples still trickling in through the doors and left them to sit down and chatter amongst themselves for the few minutes left before she got things underway.

First-time parents to be were all the same, she thought, earwigging on a conversation about how Cliona was sure she was having Braxton Hicks and Lisa's ankles were swollen. Their spouses sat with an arm draped protectively around their respective female like primitive cavemen with concern etched on their faces. They always thought they were the first human beings in the world to have procreated. Women had been suffering with the fat ankles for centuries and as for Braxton Hicks, well Cliona would know all about it when the real ones kicked in. Each generation was getting more precious than the last when it came to the practice of birthing.

Ah, speaking of precious, here was Moira looking fit to burst. Yvonne didn't fancy her chances of a natural childbirth, she'd be the sort sucking on the gas mask for all it was worth, she thought, watching her waddling in.

The conversation, which had been like the gentle humming of bees, stilled. Moira's arrival saw all the women in the room forget about blood pressure, ankles and backache. It was that special time of the week looked forward to with eager anticipation.

Tom time.

It was a treat as good as chocolate but without even more added weight gain to admire that ripe peach bottom of his beneath the denim of his jeans as he fussed around Moira getting her comfortable. It was wholesome titillation before the birthing talk began and they remembered they'd sworn off the how's your father.

The cavemen all sat with arms folded across their chests, scowls on their faces while Tom carried on, oblivious to the effect his derriere was having on the room full of hormones.

A murmur of discontent swept the room now as no Tom appeared. One woman forgot where she was momentarily and was about to demand her money back as, instead of the handsome Irish man, a woman who looked very much like Moira only older trotted in after her. Three other girls followed and to rub further salt into their wounds, they had flat stomachs. All five women were in matching yoga pants.

Moira turned her attention to Yvonne. 'I'm sorry I'm after bringing so many people with me this week, Yvonne, but they insisted. This is my mammy. Mammy, Yvonne. She's in charge.' Moira eyeballed her mammy to make sure she understood. She'd given her strict instructions that she was not to use her antenatal class as a Mo-pant marketing opportunity or else she'd tell her little babby, Nana had tried to cash in on him or her before they'd even taken their first breath. There was to be NO lunging during the hour-and-a-half-long class.

Mammy had still insisted they all wear the Mo-pant nonetheless and if anybody asked as to where they could purchase a pair of the super comfy pants then she could hardly be accused of making money off her future grandchild. She had, however, promised reluctantly not to demonstrate her moves in them.

Now she puffed up importantly. 'Hello there, Yvonne. It's lovely to meet the woman who's been preparing my daughter for giving birth. You'll be pleased to know she's taking it all very seriously. I called in to see her yesterday and she was practising the nappy folding with a tea towel. Between you and me though,' Maureen leaned in and whispered conspiratorially, 'my money is on her using the disposables. She's very squeamish when it comes to dealing with the number twos is Moira. Sure, I can't even get her to take the doggy bag with her to pick up after my poodle when she takes him for a walk. I don't know how she'll manage scraping a nappy.'

'Mammy! Yvonne doesn't want to hear all that.'

'Sorry,' Maureen didn't look in the least contrite as she added, 'Now then, Yvonne, I'm after having had four myself so if you need a hand up here then you've only got to sing out.'

'Erm, thank you.'

Maureen moved aside and another very similar woman only younger appeared. 'I'm Rosi, Yvonne. Moira's big sister. I'm training to be a yoga teacher so I've given Moira loads of breathing tips to help with the labour. I'm happy to demonstrate them for you tonight if you'd like?'

'Er, thank you, Rosi. I'll let you know if we've time.'

'And, I'm Aisling,' a woman with reddish-blonde hair who looked nothing like the other three piped up. 'Moira's middle sister. I'm not pregnant myself but I've high hopes of being in the family way soon enough so I thought I'd come along tonight and get the heads-up on what to expect.'

Yvonne smiled at her. She was certainly dedicated she thought, watching as she produced paper and pen.

'I shall be taking notes,' Aisling added.

Yet another woman stepped forth. 'My name's Andrea. I'm here in my capacity as Moira's best friend.'

'And do you have any special services to offer, Andrea?' Yvonne asked suspiciously.

'No not me, but I brought some of my mammy's chocolate slice for everyone.' She held up a Tupperware container. A calm descended smoothing the discontent in the room at the sight of the container filled with homemade chocolatey goodness.

'Right, well, now we've all met it's time we began. There's some more chairs stacked over there against the wall if you'd like to sort yourselves out.'

Moira took a seat and Andrea sat next to her on her right while Maureen, Rosi and Aisling retrieved the extra chairs.

'That waistcoat,' Andrea leaned in to whisper to Moira with a shudder, 'is hurting my eyeballs. There's no chance of her getting run over in that.'

'I told you so. Last week's was worse,' Moira whispered back, settling herself into her seat with her arms around her beach ball belly.

''Tis exciting being a part of all this,' Maureen announced to no one in particular as Roisin tugged at her sweater and told her to sit down.

Once they were seated, Yvonne welcomed them all and announced they'd begin their evening because they'd a lot to be getting through.

'It's not my first grandbabby, Rosi here's got Noah who's five.' Maureen startled the couple seated in front of her by poking her head in between them.

Yvonne fixed Maureen with a stare that told her to quieten down and everything went well for the first fifteen minutes until Moira had to elbow her mammy.

'Sit still, would you. I'm trying to concentrate.'

'I'm not after doing anything.' Maureen was indignant as she shuffled around in her seat once more.

Moira knew the signs and she leaned across and tapped Roisin on the arm. 'Tell her to behave herself. You promised me if I let you all come you'd make sure she didn't embarrass me tonight. Sure, she was a nightmare at the baby shower.'

The party had been a low-key affair organised by Aisling. Moira hadn't been bothered about having one until she'd learned presents were involved.

Roisin had flown over for it not wanting to miss out and had stayed on for a few extra days so as she could come along tonight. She'd promised to come back with Noah in tow when the baby was born. Noah was desperate to meet his new cousin and, according to Noah, so too was Mr Nibbles.

The party was also the first time Mrs Daly had met Maureen. Moira had hissed at her mammy to stop being so competitive because the guess the belly size game was just that, a game. It wasn't a sign that she was destined to be favourite nana. Had her mammy listened—no she had not— and you'd have thought she'd taken gold for Ireland the way she'd carried on. It was mortifying so it was, and Moira was determined not to have a repeat performance this evening.

'Who's she, the cat's mother?' Maureen sniffed.

'Mammy, c'mon now, be good,' Roisin whispered, knowing full well she was wasting her breath. Mammy was a law unto herself.

Aisling glanced up from where she'd been taking notes to see what was going on and recognised the bubbling-up look on her mammy's face. Poor Moira, she thought briefly, before carrying on with her nappy folding diagram.

'Sure, I don't know what either of you is on about. I'm sitting here quiet as a mouse, so I am.'

'Shush,' a big blonde girl said behind them. 'I can't hear.'

Maureen bristled. It was too much; she couldn't contain herself. The need to butt in was overwhelming. She put her hand up, ignoring Moira's glare. 'Excuse me, Yvonne. It's a grand job you're after doing putting the nappy on the wee babby there but I'd like to know what that machine does.'

'The TENS machine is a natural form of pain relief, Maureen. We'll get to it shortly if you'll bear with me.'

Maureen made a pooh-poohing noise. 'These young ones don't know they're born. In my day when you went into labour, you squeezed your eyes shut and got busy.' She looked about the room. 'I had four babbies each with a bigger pumpkin head than the last without so much as a sniff of the gas. You'll all be grand, so you will.'

'Mammy, I did not have a big pumpkin head,' Moira stated. 'Don't be telling everybody I did.'

Maureen mouthed, 'She did, enormous it was.' She held her hands open to demonstrate just how big.

'Well, good for you, Maureen, but everybody's birth story is different, that's why it's good for expectant parents to be aware of all their options.'

There was a consensus of nodding around the room.

'What does it stand for, TENS?' Rowena asked, eyeing it. She was all for pain relief.

Yvonne sighed, figuring if you couldn't beat them you might as well join them. She moved the baby doll to one side and laid a hand on top of the machine. 'Transcutaneous, Electrical, Nerve, Stimulation. It can help in different ways. For instance, it can stop pain messages from reaching your brain, and it may help trigger endorphins and improve blood circulation.'

'Is it good for the back pain, Yvonne?' Maureen asked, having put up her hand but not waited to be asked to speak.

'Yes, it can help.'

Maureen was up out of her seat before anyone could stop her. 'I suffer the backache so I do. I'm happy to be experimented on seeing as it's for a good cause.'

'It's tried and tested, Maureen, not experimental.'

And so it was, Maureen wound up with white electrode pads stuck to her back because Yvonne figured it was only the way to shut her up. Indeed, she did sit quietly only twitching when Yvonne, thinking she looked like she might interrupt, turned the stimulation modes up to high wattage. Thus she successfully finished the rest of her nappy talk.

Andrea elbowed Moira to stand up when Yvonne asked for a volunteer to demonstrate how to put on a cloth nappy and that's when it happened. As Moira got awkwardly to her feet she felt a tiny pop and then a gush of wetness. 'Mammy!' she yelped.

'Don't interrupt me when I'm on the TENS machine, Moira,' Maureen replied through clenched teeth. It was quite intense all this pulsating pain relief she thought.

'But, Mammy, I'm after wetting my knickers!'

Maureen was like the incredible hulk, she was even wearing green, as she broke free of her electrodes to stride across the room to her daughter's side. 'Moira's waters have broken. Stand back, everybody, stand back...'

Chapter Thirty-four

Bronagh was anxiously munching her way through her custard creams. Moira was in labour. Maureen had telephoned first thing to say she'd had a whoopsie at the antenatal class and had been pushing and panting ever since.

All the guests had been informed of the momentous event unfolding as they trooped down for breakfast, and staff and guests alike were on tenterhooks waiting for news.

Would it be a baby girl as Maureen predicted or a baby boy?

Bronagh didn't mind either way so long as the baby was healthy. It had been ever so long since she'd held a little baby, she couldn't wait.

The telephone shrilled into life and Bronagh hastily chewed and swallowed feeling the dried biscuit scratch her throat on the way down.

Her voice was husky as she answered with her customary greeting, her face brightening upon hearing Leonard's voice down the line. He was a welcome distraction from the interminable waiting.

'Moira's gone into labour,' she announced before he could get a word in edgewise. She listened while he made the appropriate excited noises before getting to the reason behind his call.

'I can't get hold of Joanie, Bronagh. I wanted to know how she got on yesterday with her visit.'

Leonard had not been best pleased when he'd found out Bronagh had taken matters into her own hands where his sister was concerned. That was months ago now though and Bronagh had sorted him out good and proper. She'd given him what for and he'd hung his head while she hammered home some truths.

'You've not done right by Joan, Lenny. You've let her down but it's not too late to start helping her.'

'But I don't know what to do, Bronagh, if I did I would've done it.'

Bronagh had sighed because it wasn't rocket science. 'Be there for her, show her you care without going on at her. That's all you have to do.'

Now she said, 'It went very well. Joan liked her and says she feels it's going to be a very good thing indeed.' Bronagh had tracked down a psychiatrist who specialised in talk therapy which was recommended in treating illnesses like Joan's. She was booked in for weekly sessions and Leonard was footing the bill. 'It'll be baby steps, Lenny, but she'll get there because she's taken the first one now and that's always the hardest. 'She's getting on very well with Gordon too. Friday night dinner at his place has become a regular thing.'

'I liked him when I met him. He seems a good fella.'

'He's a grand fella, Leonard. Sure, look at what's happened.'

'My sister's going to be a published photographer.'

Bronagh smiled, hearing the pride in his voice. 'She is indeed, all thanks to Gordon.'

Joan had taken a stack of her photographs around to show Gordon that first Friday and he'd gotten very excited over them. He happened to have a brother whose son worked in the publishing industry and he'd asked if he could show him the prints. Joan had been reluctant and, according to Gordon, a tug-o-war had ensued over the photographs which he'd won. He was determined Joan shouldn't hide her light under a bushel.

Things had snowballed after that with an offer of publication of Joan's collection of life on the streets of Dublin, which she accepted after a strong nudge from her brother, Bronagh, and Gordon. It would be in the shops next year pitched toward the coffee table book market.

Bronagh had acted very knowledgeable upon hearing this but she hadn't a clue what a coffee table book market was.

'And did Maureen's apartment settle on time?'

With the excitement of Moira, Bronagh had almost forgotten this other exciting news. Donal's house had sold and settled a month before but there'd been drama with the sale of Maureen's apartment. It had been touch and go as to whether the purchaser would get their loan but the bank had come to the party and it was now officially a done deal. Maureen and Donal were in the process of packing their former lives up to move into their new home and begin a new life together. It was all very romantic, Bronagh thought wistfully. She was very much hoping for a housewarming.

She chatted away to Leonard until a guest appeared asking for news of O'Mara's newest addition of which there was still none. She didn't want to tie the phone line up any longer in case Maureen was trying to ring and so she said her goodbyes.

MOIRA GAVE ONE FINAL push and a cheer went up along with a squalling cry.

Tom and Maureen had been engaged in an elbowing match since the baby's head had crowned but as Tom was handed his baby, swaddled in a towel, having done the cutting of the cord honours Maureen took a step back to allow him and Moira their moment.

Roisin, sporting a red mark on her arm where Moira had slapped her, having had enough of her sister showing her how she should be breathing, was busy helping pick Aisling up off the floor. The appearance of the little pumpkin head had all been too much for her and she'd fainted.

Tom beamed proudly down at Moira who'd been a trooper and placed their newborn daughter on her chest.

Maureen looked on her face a picture of pride and adoration before hugging Roisin and a pale-faced Aisling to her.

'A brand new O'Mara,' she whispered. 'Now then, you two, have you thought about a name because I rather like the sound of—'

The End

A Baby at O'Mara's

Book 10 - The Guesthouse on the Green
Out May 28, 2021

Printed in Great Britain
by Amazon